Female Agents

Female Agents

Laurent Vachaud

translated by Steven Rendall

BOOKS

REVOLVER BOOKS

Published by Revolver Films Ltd

Revolver Entertainment Ltd, 10 Lambton Place, Notting Hill Gate, London W11 2SH

First published in Great Britain in 2008 by Revolver Books an imprint of
Revolver Entertainment Ltd, Registered Offices: Craven House,
16 Northumberland Avenue, London WC2N 5AP

Translated from the French, *Les Femmes de l'ombre*
© 2008 Librairie Académique Perrin

Translation © Steven Rendall, 2008

Laurent Vachaud has asserted his right under the Copyright, Designs and Patents Act,
1988 to be identified as the author of this work.

ISBN: 978-1-905978-12-0

A CIP Catalogue record for this book is available from the British Library

Text design and typesetting by Dexter Haven Associates Ltd, London
Printed and Bound by CPI Group Ltd.

www.revolverbooks.com

This novel is based on the original scenario written by Jean-Paul Salomé and Laurent Vachaud for the film *Les Femmes de l'ombre* (2008).

The SOE (Special Operations Executive) and the Resistance movement in the French department of Ain took an active part in defeating the Nazi occupation forces during the Second World War. The names of their leaders mentioned in this book are authentic. Although sometimes inspired by real persons, the other characters are fictitious. This is a novel.

L.V.

Louise

Her face expressionless, Louise was ready. She'd taken her position on the footbridge looking down on the railway yard in Bourg-en-Bresse, and was waiting feverishly for Claude's signal. Despite the darkness, through her rifle's telescopic sight she could clearly discern her husband's silhouette; he was wearing the lucky cap he always wore on difficult missions. Alongside him, two other members of the Resistance – or Maquisards, as they were called – were placing plastic explosives under a locomotive. Once their task was finished they would run the wires to their hiding place about twenty metres away. Only then would they push the detonator button.

The explosion would wake up half the town and be another heavy blow to the Wehrmacht. For the past three months the Resistance in Ain had been carrying out offensive actions against the occupying forces. Panicked by these almost daily attacks in a new sector of the department, the Germans were taking vengeance by carrying out bloody reprisals against the local population. In spite of everything, the people remained completely loyal to the Maquisards.

Two days earlier, on 8 April 1944, a family had been brutally executed in the public square in La Rivoire, a small village near Champagne-en-Valromey. A bicycle suspected of belonging to a Maquisard had been found leaning against the house of the unfortunate family. Louise happened to be in the village on that day. She'd seen the father, the mother and their three children kneeling alongside one another at the command of a German officer. The officer then moved behind them and put bullets in the napes of their necks. The little girl had tried to run away; she was shot in the back and then dragged by her hair and deposited next to the bodies of her family. Their bodies had been nailed up on the doors of the family's barn and exposed to view for three days and three nights before people were allowed to take them down and bury them. It turned out that the bicycle belonged to a road-mender who was passing through the village, and that the Germans knew it from the outset. The killing was meant to serve as an example. Louise could still see the faces of the three children and the nails that pierced their wrists. That evening, if she had to fire and shed blood, she knew that she would be doing it in part to avenge the martyrs of La Rivoire.

Louise and her husband had agreed that when a patrol came along, Claude would hold up his fingers to show how many soldiers there were. Louise was to let them come as close as possible before opening fire. She was the best shot in their group, as she had already proven and as she would prove again this evening. How many Germans had she killed? Eight? Nine? She couldn't say exactly. On the other hand, she remembered very well the face of the first one she had killed, a young soldier who couldn't have been even twenty years old. That night, from the roof of the Etoile des Alpes, a grocery in Belley where Claude and his group had gone to get food, Louise, who was the lookout, had seen the guard coming. Maybe he hadn't noticed anything suspicious, maybe he just suddenly craved something to eat, who knows? Louise hadn't waited to find out, and had put two bullets in his head. 'One bullet is never enough,' Claude had said. 'Always shoot twice.'

Louise shivered. The church bell in Bourg-en-Bresse had just rung midnight. Her rifle-sight still aimed at the freight train, she couldn't help thinking that the day that was about to dawn was her birthday. She was going to be thirty-five. Should she take this as an omen? But Louise wasn't superstitious; she believed only in actions, here and now.

Lost in her thoughts, Louise didn't notice the rumbling of the vehicles until she saw Claude raise both his hands, his fingers spread wide apart. Eight. She immediately pivoted her weapon to the right, where she saw the patrol, no more than a hundred and fifty metres away. There was an armoured car in front, with a soldier in the open turret. Then came two men on a motorcycle and sidecar and a car with five soldiers aboard.

Louise waited until she had the soldier in the turret clearly in her line of sight and then pulled the trigger twice. Hit in the forehead, the man was thrown backwards. The patrol stopped dead, and she heard shouts. But she had already reloaded and, holding her breath, she fired again, taking out the motorcycle rider and his passenger. Claude and his friends took advantage of the patrol's panic to put the rest of the explosives under the last locomotive. Then they furtively moved out of the shadows and dispersed, drawing the attention of the Germans, who immediately fired on them.

The Maquisards fired back with the weapons they had hidden under their coats. As the gunfire crackled, piercing the dark like brief lightning bolts, Louise saw her husband crumple, his hand to his thigh. Claude tried to crawl under the train, but the Germans were already upon him like birds of prey. They pulled him out roughly and forced him to kneel. Her heart pounding, Louise knew that they would not kill him on the spot. When you capture the head of a group of Maquisards, you don't kill him until you've made him talk. He would be interrogated, tortured too, despite what they might have promised him in exchange for his 'cooperation'. But Louise wasn't going to let them get that far. She had reloaded her weapon and was already taking aim. The four helmeted heads appeared in her telescopic sight. Her finger was on the trigger when she heard an exclamation behind her. She felt the barrel of a weapon press against her neck. A soldier had managed to reach the footbridge and had his rifle on her, shouting words she couldn't understand. On the Nazi's face, Louise saw both his delight at having captured the isolated sniper and his astonishment on seeing that she was a woman. It was his moment of confusion that saved her life.

The man ordered her to put down her rifle and stand up. As he reached out to grab her by the hair, Louise took the knife that she kept in her sleeve and plunged it with all her strength into his neck. The soldier fell to one knee, his face still showing surprise. He tried to cry out, but could produce nothing but a sort of gurgle. His throat filled with blood and he suffocated before he could even close his hand on the handle of the knife. Louise kicked him away, removed his weapon, and got back in position.

Down on the tracks, Claude was still surrounded by the four Germans, who were searching his pockets. No one had heard what had happened on the footbridge. Claude's head was down, but Louise could tell that he was looking for her. Even if he couldn't see her clearly from where he was, he must have picked her out in the gloom, because he nodded. Although her heart was beating wildly, Louise took her time, aiming carefully at the armed man closest to her husband. She held her breath and pulled the trigger twice. The target crumpled, hit in the forehead.

The others didn't have time to react before she had already hit a second one. They panicked, and Louise took aim at a third soldier, who seemed to guess where the shots were coming from and threw himself under a freight wagon. Taking advantage of the confusion, Claude had fallen to the ground and grabbed a submachine-gun. Once he had the weapon in his hands, he turned over to shoot, but was riddled by enemy fire. Louise heard the shots at the moment that she was trying to hit the soldier hidden under the freight wagon. Without taking her eye from the sight, she turned her weapon in the direction of her husband, whom she saw hit a second time by still more lethal shots. She cried out so loudly that the man who had just fired immediately spotted her. Turning a torch on her, he began barking orders. At the same moment Louise noticed a noise. Her victim's submachine-gun, which she had laid on the footbridge, was beginning to vibrate. A rumbling was coming nearer; a new cohort of Germans had just arrived. This time, Louise could never kill them all. She took a last glance at Claude, whose lucky cap was lying a few metres from his body, and then fled.

When she got to the bottom of the footbridge, Louise took the main road, where she found the railwayman who had given them access to the locomotives. Perfectly calm despite the tumult all around them, he had been joined by Fanfan, one of the Maquisards who had helped Claude put the explosives under the trains. Fanfan had succeeded in escaping, but didn't realize that he was the only survivor.

'You can't take the lorry, there'll be roadblocks everywhere. Follow me,' the railwayman said. They hurried but did not run. In the distance the sound of dogs barking grew louder.

'Claude?' Fanfan asked Louise. She just shook her head. He didn't ask anything else. When they arrived in front of a building with a blackened façade, the railwayman knocked twice on the door, then knocked again, more slowly, three times. His wife let them in without a word. The railwayman led Louise into the kitchen, where the rest of the family was finishing the evening meal, despite the late hour. The grandmother, grandfather and sister kept their eyes on them, at the same time continuing to eat their soup. The railwayman pushed aside the dog's mat to reveal a trap door.

'We have to warn Chabot,' Louise said.

'He's supposed to come tomorrow. I'll bring some soup down to you in a minute.' He opened the trap door. A wooden stairway went down into the cellar. Louise went first, followed by Fanfan, who closed the trap door behind him. The railwayman put the mat back in its place and sat down at the table with his family, as if nothing had happened.

Louise and Fanfan remained silent, each stretched out at one end of the cellar. German patrols had moved through the area without searching the houses. Nonetheless, Fanfan was very nervous; he kept turning over on the old mattress that served as his bed, replaying the events he had just experienced. He sensed that Louise was not sleeping either, but seemed to be ignoring him. She hadn't said a word to him since she'd come back. Maybe she was punishing him for having left Claude to the Germans. He'd been afraid, true, he was prepared to admit that much. Yes, his first concern was to save his own skin. Was he going to have to pay for that?

Louise had intimidated him ever since the first time he'd seen her, not just because she was twelve years older than him, but because her face never betrayed her thoughts. She'd impressed even the Germans. He remembered the day that she'd been stopped at a roadblock with radio parts tied around her waist. She'd been searched by a young soldier, who let her go even though he'd felt the metal objects under her blouse. Fanfan had long wondered why. Maybe he was only looking for a pistol, and had paid no attention to what he took to be a large belt. Or maybe he was in a hurry to finish his work on that hot afternoon; he'd already checked hundreds of people. But for Fanfan there was another explanation: the guard had looked into Louise's eyes, and the impassiveness of her face had convinced him that there was no point in holding her any longer.

When Fanfan first met Louise, she was a nurse in the hospital at Nantua. He and Claude were carrying out a raid on the hospital to get medicines and bandages to take back to the Morez camp. While they were in the storeroom and Claude was throwing bottles and boxes into a large bag, Fanfan had heard steps out in the corridor. Holding their pistols, they saw the door open, and a woman with a Madonna-like face looked in. 'You could have asked,' she said in her most inexpressive fashion. 'You'd have saved time.' Without saying another word, she led them to another room where powerful pain-killers were stored; she put the bottles in their bags herself.

As they were leaving with ten times as many medical supplies as they had expected, Claude turned to Louise and said, 'Why don't you come with us? You'd save time, too.' Fanfan would have sworn that three seconds before Claude uttered those words he'd had no idea what he was going to say. It just popped out, because she was she, and he was he. Louise looked at him silently for a moment, then took off her nurse's cap and followed them. That was how it had all begun, on the night of 10 November 1942 at the hospital in

7

Nantua. Two months later, Claude got the mayor to come out to the Morez farm and marry them. Louise was not a believer, and didn't want a religious ceremony. Fanfan served as a witness for Claude, and Etienne for Louise. He didn't know where she came from or whether she still had family members in the region. She never talked about them.

'I'm not angry with you, you know.' Fanfan realized that Louise had just spoken to him. In the semi-darkness, he could just make out that she was looking at him; she'd taken down her hair, and that made her look less severe. 'You think I'm angry at you because of Claude,' she went on. 'That's not true. I was supposed to cover you, and I wasn't quick enough, it's all my fault. Try to sleep, tomorrow is another day.'

Tomorrow is another day. This woman had seen her husband killed in front of her eyes, she felt a terrible sense of guilt, and she managed to say, 'Tomorrow is another day.' Even if she made a show of remaining impervious, she loved Claude more than her own life, and his death must have been devastating for her. Nonetheless, there she was, a few metres away, completely calm and in control of herself. Fanfan was only twenty-three, but he thought he'd never meet anyone as unique as Louise Desfontaines.

The future was to prove him right. Three days later, on the Hotonnes plateau, while returning to the fortified camp of Abergement, he was surprised by a Wehrmacht patrol. To make a point, the Germans decapitated him, along with five other Maquisards who had accompanied him. Louise had left France the day before, and never learned that Fanfan had joined Claude on the long list of the martyrs of Valromey.

'They've identified Claude. Your photo is being circulated throughout the region. By staying here, you'd be putting the whole group in danger. You've got to leave.' Louise looked at the man who had just spoken to her. Heavy-set, of average height, Henri Romans-Petit was the head of the Maquis in Ain, or was at least the only superior she recognized. A veteran of the First World War, he had been one of the first to reject the armistice signed in June 1940, though he had not been able to get to London. He was exceptionally courageous and dashing, and had gained fame by organizing the raid on the Youth Labour Service group in Artemare, carried out to equip the Maquis with clothing and footwear. Later on, he had defied the Germans by marching a column of Maquisards right through the centre of Oyonnax on 11 November 1943.

Romans-Petit was like a big brother to Claude and Louise. He had to be, despite the fact that they always used the formal *vous* in addressing each other. But if she disapproved of one of his orders at first, she knew that she would always end up giving in. At his side was Henri Girousse, called Chabot, the commander of the Southern Group, which included several camps of Maquisards that had been organized on the Hotonnes and Hauteville plateaus. Shortly before dawn, Chabot had come looking for Fanfan and Louise at the railwayman's house. He already knew about Claude, but did not let his grief show. The three of them drove for more than an hour in the most complete silence before stopping at the Corlier camp, to which Louise and Fanfan were attached. She was getting out of the car when Chabot suddenly said to her, 'Louise, you're going on with me as far as Brénod. He wants to talk to you.'

She froze. 'He's there?'

'He just wants to talk to you.'

When the Maquisards said 'he', they meant Romans-Petit. He was waiting for them down the road, at the Fort farm in Brénod. Like all the leaders of the Resistance, Romans and Chabot never spent more than twenty-four hours together in the same group. Meetings at set times were even rarer. If the two men were breaking that rule, it was because the situation was serious, Louise knew that much. Like Chabot, when he was face-to-face with Louise, Romans avoided mentioning Claude. Instead, he told her that they had decided to attack a train that would have been put out of commission by the sabotage attempt at Bourg-en-Bresse, had it succeeded. Chabot was still not sure who he wanted to lead the attack, which was to take place the same day. When Louise volunteered for the job, Romans refused; he no longer wanted her in the region, she had to leave.

'I can't fight any more if I go away,' she pleaded.

'You're going to Spain, and from there you'll be taken to a camp, where you'll wait for transfer to England.'

That sounded like the worst of punishments. Romans turned the knife in the wound: 'Over there, you can continue the fight, Louise. They'll find a good way to make use of you.'

Louise shook her head; she was determined to stand up to him this time. 'They'll put me behind a desk, you mean. I belong in the field, you know that very well. After what happened here, I'll accept any assignment at all, and if you want to punish me, give me the most dangerous one you've got, even if I have to do it alone, I've nothing left to lose. Just don't send me to England!'

'No one's trying to punish you, Louise. You had no way of knowing that the enemy had doubled the troops at the station.

Chabot and I take full responsibility for what happened yesterday.'

'We're sending you to London because that's where you can be most useful. What you know will be of great help to them,' Chabot said.

'But I don't know anyone over there! How could I help anyone?'

'Pierre is working for the SOE; he'll know where you should be assigned.'

Louise stared at the two men, incredulous. 'Pierre? Pierre who?'

'Pierre Desfontaines, your brother.'

Chabot's reply stunned her. 'My brother, in England? That's ridiculous, you don't know him, his views are the same as my father's, and besides, he's much too cowardly to ... '

Romans cut her short: 'One of our liaison agents told us that he'd been trained in London under the command of a certain Pierre Desfontaines, who'd been with the SOE since February 1943. When did you last speak with your brother, Louise?'

Chabot was looking at her now with a faint smile.

'In December 1942.'

The two men exchanged a knowing look.

'No one is as simple as he seems, Louise. You didn't know your brother as well as you thought you did.'

For the first time, Louise didn't know what to say to Romans.

Pierre

Baker Street had always been evocative for him.

He imagined himself a teenager again, sitting on the stairs of the family château, devouring a new adventure of Sherlock Holmes. Under his breath, he repeated the names: Baskerville, Moriarty, Baker Street; they were like so many passports to the land of dreams.

If a detective living in Baker Street could defeat the most dangerous adversaries imaginable, what could a secret service lodged in the same street be expected to do? The offices of the Special Operations Executive were unprepossessing. They had first been located in Caxton Street, near St James's Park, and had moved to Holmes's territory when they requisitioned the former offices of Marks & Spencer. Operating under the name 'Inter-Services Research Bureau', they now occupied as many as six buildings in the street. For more than a year and a half, Pierre had been working in the French section, called 'Section F', which was led by Colonel Maurice Buckmaster, a man with a pendulous lip and a phlegmatic disposition who knew how to size up a person at first glance. However, up to this point Pierre thought he'd managed to conceal a whole side of his life from the Colonel, and he was rather proud of that.

He still remembered his first encounter with Buck. A few weeks after landing in Scotland, he'd arrived in London, where a contact had told him there was a new office that was recruiting Frenchmen: the SOE. Created by Winston Churchill and set up by the Minister for Economic Warfare, Hugh Dalton, the SOE had as its mission to carry out sabotage against enemy installations on the continent. This goal had awakened Pierre's romantic streak, and he was one of the first to arrive at Section F, where he was received by a recruiting agent named Selwyn Jepson. By an extraordinary coincidence, Jepson was the author of several spy novels that Pierre had read and liked, and this made it easy for the two men to get on with each other. The fact that Pierre was an officer in the French army was also a point in his favour, and Jepson highly recommended him. After that, he had to get through an interview with the head of the office himself: Colonel Buckmaster.

'You went to Saint-Cyr, I see,' said Buck in perfect French, lighting his pipe.

'Yes, sir.'

'A family tradition?'

'No, sir. My father was a professor.'

'Do you still have family in France?'

'My father, yes.'

'Your mother is deceased?'

'Yes, sir, when I was twelve.'

'Brothers and sisters?'

Pierre hesitated for a moment. 'No, sir.'

Buck scribbled a few words on a notepad.

'What can you tell me about your father?'

Pierre squirmed on his chair. 'He was the Rector of the University of Lyons ... We lived there until my mother died. Then he preferred to live in the family château, near Nantua.'

'Does he know that you're in England?'

'No, sir, he doesn't.'

'You left without telling him?'

'Let's say that I left after an argument with him.'

'What were you arguing about?'

'My father is very conservative. He's always thought the defeat was legitimate. And he has absolute confidence in Pétain.'

'And you didn't?'

Pierre looked around at the office in which he was sitting. On a low table near the window there was a chess set. Every time Buck asked a question, he felt as if a piece had been moved on the board.

'I had personal reasons to think differently.'

'Which were?'

Pierre took a deep breath. 'The Germans killed my fiancée.'

Buck took a few more notes. Pierre was amazed by his own audacity. The words had popped out by themselves before he'd had time to think.

Buck had never again asked why he had volunteered, and Pierre had thought this showed that his little lie had been successful. That is why on this May morning, as he entered Buck's office to tell him that a radio operator had reappeared in Meudon, he felt the ground crumble beneath him when the colonel barked, 'Why didn't you tell me you had a sister?'

Buck showed him a search bulletin put out by the Gestapo; it bore a photo of Louise Granville, née Desfontaines. Like a little boy caught in a lie, Pierre could only look down at his feet.

'If she had supported Vichy like your Father, I could understand,' Buck went on. 'But she's a model Resistance fighter, recommended by Lieutenant-Colonel Romans-Petit.'

'It's a long story …' Pierre stammered.

Buck opened a file folder on the desk in front of him. 'The story I read is rather short. Your sister escaped to Spain after the death of her husband during an operation. Claude Granville, a first-rate Maquisard, a member of the Corlier group...'

'Yes, I know...'

'She spent three weeks in the Miranda camp. That was where she let the Red Cross know that she wanted to join our office. Our consul gave her an exit permit. She left Gibraltar this morning.'

'Colonel, I know what you're thinking, but let me say that...'

'You never had a fiancée who was killed by the Germans, right?'

Pierre felt himself blush. 'No.'

'Then why did you lie to me?'

'My life seemed rather dull, and I wanted to liven it up.'

'This time your lie isn't very convincing.'

'If you will permit me to say so, Colonel, I don't think Louise would be useful in our office.'

'And why not? You're as aware as I am that we need more people in Section F.'

'My sister is very unpredictable...'

'Excellent! That's how wars are won, as you know.'

'But she's a hothead, she rejects any kind of authority.'

'Very well. We'll make her an officer.'

Pierre gave in. He was beaten. Buck smiled slightly.

'Her boat arrives in Scotland tomorrow. She'll be flown immediately to the military airfield in Aldershot. Can I count on you to bring her here?'

Pierre nodded, and left the colonel's office.

The following day, on the road to Aldershot, Pierre wondered why he'd hidden Louise's existence from Buck. Through the wipers sweeping the rain from his windscreen, he saw the face of Édouard Véry. He and Édouard had been born in the same year, and had been schoolmates before undergoing military training at Saint-Cyr. During the Christmas holiday, Édouard was alone at the school, because his family was then living abroad, where his father was serving as a police officer. Pierre always invited him to spend Christmas Eve with his family at their château in Le Bérail. Pierre's father became so fond of Édouard that he practically considered him his second son. Édouard met Louise at Le Bérail, but they lost touch with each other when she went to study philosophy in Lyons. At the time, Louise looked like a real tomboy, with her short hair, and she was always ready to play football with them on the poorly maintained grounds of the château. On Christmas Eve 1938, Édouard did not expect to see the gloriously feminine young woman with long hair who greeted him with a simple 'Hello Édouard, how are you?' as if they'd seen each other only the day before. During the meal, Pierre had found himself blushing when Louise asked him personal questions. He saw that Édouard liked her but was too shy to tell her how he felt. After dinner, Pierre went to his sister's room.

'You know,' he said to her, 'I think Édouard really likes you.'

'I like him too, he's very nice.'

'No, I mean I think he's in love with you.'

Louise was sitting in front of her mirror, putting her hair in a bun. Without even turning around, she replied, 'You do? How cute.'

She said nothing more. Over the following days, Pierre did all he could to bring them together. Things followed their usual course, and a few months later, Édouard asked Louise's father for her hand in marriage, and his request was granted.

'I'm very happy that you're joining our family, Édouard,' Monsieur Desfontaines said, 'and I think you'll be very good for Louise.' He thought that Louise needed to be set back on the right path. In the spring of 1939, she'd announced that she was not going to pursue the academic career he had in mind for her.

'I feel no vocation, and besides, those professors are all so boring. I don't want to be like them.'

Her father naturally took this to mean 'I don't want to be like you.' He repeatedly tried to change her mind, but always ran into the same wall. Louise wanted to be a nurse, because she thought that would be more useful, and moreover something that no one else in her family did – a consideration that was not without importance for her. Her father was counting on Édouard to persuade her to return to the study of philosophy. Édouard assured him that he could manage it before the marriage, which was to take place in early July. But in the last week of June, Louise surprised everyone again when she declared that she no longer wanted to marry Édouard.

Monsieur Desfontaines had invited Édouard and his family to Le Bérail, where the whole third floor of the house was reserved for them. At the first dinner with the Véry family, Pierre understood that things were not looking good. Just after they finished the first course, Louise said she didn't feel well and wanted to get some fresh air. She excused herself, and an hour later she still had not returned. Édouard left the table to look for her. He did not find her. Three hours later she reappeared, but offered no explanation whatever for her absence.

That evening, as she was going up the stairs of the château to join her fiancé in his room, she whispered to Pierre, 'I don't think this is going to work, you know.' Pierre asked her what she meant. She didn't reply. The next morning she'd made up her mind. After informing Édouard, and then Pierre, she waited until everyone had gathered around the breakfast table before speaking. 'I beg you to forgive me for the pain I'm going to cause you, but I've decided not to marry Édouard. I've thought long and hard about this, and I think that it's better for everyone concerned. I'm sure Édouard will find another fiancée who will be more suitable for him. You'll see, some day you'll thank me.'

Afterward, Louise left Le Bérail, leaving the guests in a state of shock and poor Édouard inconsolable. The cancellation of the wedding greatly disturbed people in the area. Monsieur Desfontaines swore that he wouldn't allow his daughter to set foot on his property again, then fell into a depression that incapacitated him until September. Édouard's parents handled things much better; they were convinced that their ex-future daughter-in-law was a madwoman who would surely have caused their son a great deal of trouble. Édouard himself never got over this tragic event. When France went to war in May 1940, he did everything he could to be sent to the front, despite his parents, who had found him a safe job at the War Ministry. Pierre, who didn't want to let him go alone, followed him to Sedan. On the first day of fighting, Édouard was killed by enemy fire. Pierre was still convinced that he had committed suicide, and held Louise directly responsible.

When Pierre returned to Le Bérail, he was a different person. There, nothing had really changed. His father had heard nothing further from Louise, and avoided mentioning her name. Asking around the neighbourhood, Pierre learned that his sister was living in Nantua, where she was working as a nurse at the city hospital. For a moment he was tempted to go and tell her that Édouard was dead, but did not, fearing that she would react with an indifference that would only increase his anger at her. Although he was boiling with indignation and rage, he didn't let it show, and to an outside observer Pierre would have seemed simply resigned and apathetic. He didn't even feel strong enough to resist his father, who gave him a heartfelt lecture on the incompetence of the French army. However, Pierre did not accept France's surrender. But he did not hide his esteem for Marshal Pétain, who had just signed the armistice with Hitler at Compiègne. When Pierre was a student, Pétain had been his hero and had greatly impressed him during a visit to Saint-Cyr. He and Édouard would have followed the marshal to the very gates of Hell if necessary.

But now they were in Hell. Édouard was dead, and Pétain could never get them out again, though it had taken Pierre more than two years to see that. Like many other Frenchmen, he'd finally understood when he got a summons from the STO, the programme that provided forced labour for Germany. At Christmas 1942, he got into a violent quarrel with his father, who ordered him to get out immediately. Nonetheless, Pierre remained, returning to his room instead. A few hours later he'd made his decision: he would leave the family home the next day.

Pierre found a room to let in Nantua. Jean Daroz, one of his old classmates at Saint-Cyr, told him about a way of escaping to England. One evening in December, he was to meet his contact person, and just before leaving his room he heard a knocking at the window. Curious, he opened the window. A woman wearing a raincoat and a beret gestured to him. It was Louise. Although he hadn't seen her for three years, he recognized her immediately. He let her in and offered her a cup of tea.

Louise came straight to the point: 'You don't want to go to Germany, it seems?'

'Who told you that?'

'I've still got my informants in Le Bérail, you know.'

'So I see.'

'They even say that you got into a fight with Papa.'

'I thought you were the one I was fighting with. I haven't had any word from you for three years, Louise.'

'I know. But I couldn't talk to you. I thought you were like him.'

Pierre watched her sip the cup of camomile tea he had just served her. She really hadn't changed at all. 'I've got my informants too. So, you're working at the hospital in Nantua?'

'Not any more. A lot of things have happened in my life lately, you know.'

'I should think so. Did you hear about Édouard?'

'No. Did he get married?'

Pierre resisted a strong impulse to slap her. He limited himself to a cynical smile. 'He was killed in front of my eyes at Sedan. I thought you knew about it.'

'No, I didn't even know that he'd fought.'

'I'd say rather that he got himself killed. Because of you.'

'Stop it, Pierre!'

'You broke his heart, at least have the decency to acknowledge that.'

She leapt to her feet and looked him straight in the eyes. 'I can't mourn someone who got himself killed when comrades are resisting and dying all around me every day!'

'Comrades? Resisting? What are you talking about?'

She hesitated for a second, as if about to make a major admission. 'I've met a man, Pierre, a man I love and at whose side I have decided to fight. I came to ask you to join us.'

'Who is it? Do I know him?'

'His name is Claude Granville... He was a teacher in Oyonnax.'

'Granville? The communist?'

'What difference does that make? We're all fighting together now, aren't we?'

Pierre opened the door and said coldly, 'I won't fight alongside a communist. Adieu, Louise.'

She looked at him for a moment, alarmed, then set down her teacup. 'I thought you'd changed. But you're still like him.' She left the room and disappeared into the night. That same evening, Pierre met Jean Darroz. A month later, he landed in Edinburgh.

Pierre had now arrived in Aldershot. He parked his car in front of the mess hall at the Aldershot airfield, where Buck had said Louise would be waiting for him. Slightly nervous, he took a moment before getting out of the car. He hadn't seen his sister since that night in December 1942, and was apprehensive about meeting her again. She was now a widow, and had been in combat several times. For his own part, he'd carried out a few missions on French soil, had been tortured, and barely escaped death, but nothing equalling what his sister had endured in the Maquis. Louise had more experience, but she was going to have to rely on him now. Pierre wondered how they would deal with this unfamiliar situation, for despite the circumstances, he couldn't disregard the acute sense of competition that had set him against his sister all his life.

Entering the mess hall, he looked round without seeing a single familiar face. A few soldiers were playing billiards, others were lunching, but he didn't see a woman alone. He turned around to go to the bar, and it was then that he saw her, her elbows on the counter and a shy smile on her lips.

'I wasn't sure it was you. The uniform makes you look taller...' Louise's brown overcoat was thrown over her shoulders, and she was wearing a dark skirt, lace-up shoes and a brown beret that made her look like a student. The sweet look he liked so much radiated from her beautiful face. But Pierre knew that she was too volcanic to respond to sentimentality. He decided to be polite.

'I heard about your husband. I'm very sorry.'

Louise just nodded and took another sip of tea.

'How did you know that I was with the SOE?'

'Through my superiors in the Maquis. I was surprised. I thought you'd surrendered. The last time I saw you, you didn't seem very combative.'

'I didn't want to fight alongside you – that's different.'

'You didn't want to fight alongside my communist husband, and that's something else again.' She saw that she'd scored a point. 'So,' she went on, 'London was the best way to get as far away from me and from Claude as you could.'

'I couldn't understand what you saw in him, that's true.'

'You've never understood what I saw in any man who wasn't Édouard – that is, who wasn't you.' She drank the rest of her tea and looked at him. 'Shall we go?'

Stunned, Pierre realized that nothing was going to be simple.

They returned to London in almost complete silence. Pierre drove, while Louise, sitting in the back, contemplated impassively the damage the Blitz had done to the city. Her eyes lingered on a bookstore whose roof had been torn away; Londoners, indifferent to the surrounding chaos, were looking at books on the shelves that had not been destroyed. Pierre parked in front of his home, a small red-brick house not far from Baker Street. In the garden, which was overrun with weeds, there was still a sign indicating that the place was no longer to let. At the back, a dilapidated iron frame supported a rusty swing that squeaked when there was a gust of wind.

Pierre led her to the room he'd prepared for her on the second floor. On the hideous wallpaper, sheep were jumping a fence. The furnishings consisted of a bed, a small desk and chair, and a wardrobe.

'If you need another blanket, I've got some in my room,' Pierre said, opening the window.

The furniture was so disparate that Louise suspected her brother of having found it in a rubbish dump. If he'd wanted to make her feel unwanted, he had succeeded beyond his wildest dreams.

'When will you take me to the SOE?' she asked, unpacking her bag.

'Tomorrow morning. You've got an appointment with the recruiter. He's a little eccentric, as you'll see.'

'What's he going to ask me? Whether I'm motivated?'

Pierre leaned against the wall. He was observing her. 'It's just a formality, to see which office they're going to assign you to.'

'Which office?' Louise froze. The shy smile she saw on Pierre's lips was not a good omen. 'Are you saying I could end up somewhere other than in the field?'

'That's for them to decide, I can't promise you anything.'

She examined him in silence. He pushed off the wall and said to her, as he started down the stairs, 'Have a good rest. You must need it.'

The following days consisted of just what Louise had feared most: forced inactivity. After an interview that was not very eccentric, given what Pierre had led her to expect, Selwyn Jepson recommended her for a job in the temporary secretarial pool while waiting for a mission suitable for her. So she spent more than two weeks filing documents, sharpening pencils and occasionally exchanging banalities with Vera Atkins, Colonel Buckmaster's assistant. Buckmaster himself remained mysteriously inaccessible. Bored to death, Louise never passed up an opportunity to leave Section F's offices to explore the SOE's other buildings, which she wrongly imagined to be bubbling with greater activity. In spite of everything, she established contacts with other female agents who had returned from missions or were waiting for a new assignment. Fascinated, she listened to them tell about their exploits with a nostalgia for action that was all the more manifest because their feats made her bureaucratic idleness even more unbearable.

One of these young women made a strong impression on her. Hardly twenty-eight years old, Christina Granville was one of the most beautiful women she'd ever seen, and one of the last she would have imagined doing this kind of work. Although Louise was several years older, she saw herself in this energetic woman who bore the same family name as her husband and had carried out extremely dangerous missions in both Europe and Africa. In the Italian Alps, Christina had escaped from a whole detachment of German soldiers during an epic race on skis. She and her lover, a hero in the Polish army, formed a clashing pair that reminded Louise of her relationship with Claude. Even their origins were comparable: both of them had aristocratic blood in their veins. Born Krystyna Skarbek in Poland, the young woman belonged to one of the illustrious families that had driven the Teutonic Knights out of Poland in the fifteenth century. The gold ring she wore on her middle finger was divided with a band of steel in memory of those heroic times. When Louise asked her what it meant, Christina told her about an episode in which her ancestor Jan Skarbek had opposed Emperor Henry II. The Emperor, about to invade Poland, had tried to convince Skarbek that resistance was futile, showing him the coffers full of gold he was going to use to pay his army. Christina's ancestor had pulled off his ring and thrown it on the treasure, saying, 'Let gold return to gold, we Poles prefer steel.'

That day, Louise spent more than an hour listening to the Iron Lady tell her adventures. Their conversation was interrupted when Vera Atkins asked Louise to return immediately to Section F. Shaking Christina's hand, Louise told her that she would like to die having lived even a tenth of Christina's life. She had no idea what was in store for her.

Heindrich

Karl Heindrich awoke with a start. As always, he'd dreamed of Liliane. Light was filtering through his bedroom shutters. He saw that he was late, again.

Why hadn't Volker awakened him at six a.m.? He'd left strict orders. Then he remembered that he'd locked his door before going to bed. Volker had probably knocked, and might even have tried to come in. But he should have tried harder. After all, Karl could have been ill, injured, even dying, why not? If he was completed devoted to him, Volker should have been worried and broken down the door. He could no longer count on Volker. He was going to have a talk with him, and he'd better have a good excuse, or else…

Karl immediately got a grip on himself. He'd gone completely off the rails. Volker was the most reliable aide-de-camp imaginable. Heindrich knew that he himself was to blame. This business had been wearing on him for too long, and he couldn't let it get him down, especially not just now.

He had to get Liliane out of his head. He had to stop playing games with Eddy, all that nonsense that led nowhere and was distracting him from his work. He'd put an end to it today.

Karl looked at his watch: 7.10 a.m. The meeting was set for nine o'clock at General von Rundstedt's headquarters in Saint-Germain-en-Laye. Wilhelm, his driver, could make the trip in less than an hour, which meant he should leave by eight at the latest. Then he'd have an hour to review his speech. More than enough time, especially since he was in complete command of his subject, and von Rundstedt couldn't make fun of him this time.

Von Rundstedt. As he put on his uniform, Karl imagined the marshal's eagle eye. The old fool didn't pardon him any error, any imprecision. So he should strike hard, and immediately; stun them, him and his protégés. Karl glanced at himself in the mirror. He looked good, despite having slept poorly.

Someone knocked at the door. 'Colonel?'

Karl recognized Volker's voice. He strode swiftly to the door and opened it. His aide-de-camp stood there, his uniform in perfect trim, as usual. How did he manage always to be so calm and impeccable, no matter what happened?

'I was a little concerned. I came by a while ago and you didn't answer.'

'Everything is fine, Volker. Tell Wilhelm that I'll come down at eight o'clock.'

'That Eddy fellow called for you again.'

Karl stiffened. Eddy. 'What did he want?'

'He didn't go into details. He just said that he had something for you, and that he absolutely had to see you.'

Karl didn't want to hear anything more about this Eddy; he'd have to tell Volker to forbid him to come into the hotel.

Volker was waiting. 'Shall I tell him to come back, Colonel?'

'I don't have time to deal with him now – tell him he'll have to wait.' Karl closed the door, cursing his weakness.

Despite the early hour, the corridors of the Regina were bustling with activity. Since the SS's secret services had set up their headquarters in this great hotel in central Paris, the place had no rest. Heindrich would have preferred to stay at the Lutetia. When he was running the Abwehr there, he'd been able to live outside, and thus lead a more healthy life. He slept better, he benefited from a sharper distinction between his private life and his work, and his nerves failed him less often. And then the Regina reminded him so much of Liliane. Von Rundstedt surely remembered that, the bastard; he'd plotted to have Karl transferred to this new location. The marshal must have known how much it would pain him to walk up and down these corridors now that she had disappeared.

The bastard.

Von Rundstedt had taken a dislike to him the first time they met. Despite all his efforts to pull the wool over the marshal's eyes, the latter had sensed that they didn't come from the same social world. Karl hadn't been careful enough. The old fogey had read him like an open book.

Karl did not have the same status as most of the senior German commanders in Paris; he didn't belong to the upper middle class, still less to the Prussian aristocracy, like von Rundstedt. And he paid the price for that every day.

His parents, modest merchants in Dresden, had encouraged his ambitions. But he'd climbed the ladder on his own, using his own strength, without an uncle or a cousin to serve as his patron. And he'd succeeded. For example, the day when he learned that he'd been assigned to Paris. He was so proud of that. The Führer had sent him a personal letter of congratulation. The Führer didn't come from a wealthy background either, and he'd been able to see that Karl was capable, and to tell him so in simple, brotherly words. This recognition had put Karl on cloud nine. As soon as he moved into the splendid ten-room apartment on the

Boulevard Raspail that had been assigned to him, he'd decided to celebrate the event by throwing an unforgettable party. Everyone who was anyone in Paris was there, as well as the whole of the German General Staff; they'd come to witness his coronation and, above all, to see Liliane. He still remembered their faces when she appeared on his arm, radiant in a dress designed for her by Mademoiselle Chanel.

They were green with envy.

Liliane, whom they had seen dance nude at the Folies Bergère. Liliane, cause of so many fantasies. Even von Rundstedt. She belonged to Karl now. He had seduced her, not by his fortune or his origins, but by his sincerity. None of the jackals present at his party was prepared to admit that. In their view, he was just a little luckier. Towards the end of the evening, when the joyful mood was waning, Karl said to himself that the time had come to strike the coup de grâce. The generals and the marshal were getting their overcoats at the cloakroom and preparing to leave, whispering in each other's ears words that he didn't hear but could imagine only too well. 'Poor Heindrich, he thinks this little whore loves him, but tomorrow she'll be with someone else – let him have his fun while he can.'

Karl knew they were all thinking the same thing. Maybe they were even already taking bets on who would take her away from him.

The hyenas.

Then he asked for people's attention, putting a sudden stop to all conversation. Even Liliane, astonished, looked at him. She was not expecting what he was about to say. Without taking his eyes off von Rundstedt and the other generals, Heindrich came up to Liliane and told her that the seventy-eight days they had spent together were already among the finest moments of his life. Since he was hoping to share many more with her, he was choosing the occasion of this party to ask her hand in marriage. Like a child who has received a gift she has always wanted, Liliane mumbled a few words of consent. Karl still recalled the applause that had followed. They all clapped their hands and cried 'Bravo!' Even von Rundstedt had to go along. Karl had forced him to applaud.

After the guests had left, Liliane told him she didn't want to sleep in the apartment. She wanted to go to the Regina. And not to just any suite either: she wanted the one where they had first made love. That time, in room 813, Karl had felt like a child, letting himself be guided by Liliane, who allowed him to do anything he wanted, giving herself to him completely. That night he'd felt invulnerable. And yet it marked the beginning of the end.

After two months of pure happiness, the wedding was to take place in the church of Saint-Germain-des-Prés on 15 June 1942, and then to be celebrated in the Lutetia's reception rooms, where more than five hundred guests were expected. Gabrielle Chanel had made a unique dress for the bride, which Karl would see for the first time at the church. Liliane's parents being deceased, the choreographer from the Folies Bergère had offered to accompany the bride to the altar. Karl had brought his mother from Germany so that she could enter the church on his arm, her head held high – she, the grocery-woman from Dresden, gazed upon by the hyenas. But he soon perceived omens of catastrophe. Two hours before she was to say 'Yes,' the bride was still nowhere to be seen. Her maids of honour, who were all dancers at the Folies, claimed they hadn't seen her since she went into her dressing room to put on her gown. Karl sent Ulrich, a cousin and witness who had also come from Dresden, to find out what was delaying the bride. Ulrich returned three-quarters of an hour later, looking embarrassed: Liliane had simply vanished. The minutes ticked by, unbearably, until the fateful moment when Karl felt obliged to announce, in a church filled with people, that the ceremony had been cancelled. His glance intersected with that of von Rundstedt, who was affecting an impenetrable expression but was internally exultant.

The following days were among the most painful Karl had ever experienced. Holed up in his suite at the Lutetia, he continued to receive congratulatory messages from people who had been invited to the wedding but had been unable to attend, and who knew nothing about the débâcle. What had happened to Liliane? Had she been frightened at the last moment, scared by the commitment? Had she left him for someone else? He couldn't believe that. One last hypothesis obsessed him: von Rundstedt and his henchmen had killed her. He tried in vain to put the idea out of his head, telling himself that it was absurd, but it stayed with him late into the night, when he finally fell into a slumber in which Liliane still haunted him.

Ready at last, Heindrich left the hotel, followed by Volker, and got into the car. They reached Saint-Germain-en-Laye in less than forty minutes. Von Rundstedt and his personal guard were still eating lunch when Karl's arrival was announced. Cordially, they invited him to have coffee and pastries with them. He declined politely, and went to wait in the drawing room. He wasn't going to let them run things; this morning, he was going to deal the cards.

Volker seemed shocked by Karl's refusal to accept von Rundstedt's invitation, but Karl didn't feel compelled to explain. Aware that what he was to reveal represented his only chance of regaining his position, Heindrich had taken great care not to let it get out, so as to ensure that it would have the maximum impact. He wanted to surprise the group. Karl had to admit that despite the spies von Rundstedt had posted at the Regina, Volker had done a remarkable job of keeping everyone in the dark. The secrets Karl was going to divulge went beyond his personal interests; they might also mark a turning point in the war. In his view, they represented a true sign from God, the compensation for the terrible disappointments he'd had to endure over the past months. He was finally going to be able to show that he should be given another post worthy of his true merits. Von Rundstedt would be obliged to speak to the Führer himself about it, and to mention his name. From then on, everything became possible.

The old fool's secretary approached them. 'The Marshal awaits you, Colonel.'

The first photo appeared on the screen. It showed concrete cubes floating in the midst of what looked like the roads of a seaport. Using a pointer, Karl described the photo for the audience. 'This picture was taken three days ago by one of our spy planes. At the time, the pilot was over the port at Southampton. Machine-gun fire was immediately directed at him, and it's a miracle that he returned unharmed.'

At the back of the room, Karl saw von Rundstedt petting his dog. He remained unperturbed. In the first row, someone raised his hand to ask a question. 'What are those odd things in the port? They look like grain silos ...'

Two of the hyenas broke out laughing. Karl could have skinned them alive. He tried to keep his composure, and even went so far as to smile.

'Grain silos defended by anti-aircraft guns? No, I think these structures will play a crucial role in the coming invasion.'

Karl's response was met with glacial silence. The marshal continued to pet his dog. Had he said too much too soon? The old goat was still not reacting.

Karl went on with his explanations regarding the number and volume of the structures, in comparison to which the British workers looked like insignificant insects.

'As you can see, there are eight of these concrete cubes, and behind them are watchtowers and anti-aircraft batteries. I wasn't aware that grain was so well protected in England.'

That was when von Rundstedt spoke up. 'Colonel Heindrich, why are most of our divisions assembled in the region around Calais?'

Karl was expecting this question. 'Because the area around Calais has several ports where our enemies could easily land with all their equipment and supplies.'

The marshal nodded. 'And because it's also the shortest route between the English coast and the continent. Southampton isn't really right across from Calais, is it? So I don't see how your cubes could play a role in the landing.'

Karl didn't become flustered. 'Allow me to differ with you, Marshal. What if the landing in Calais were only a diversion, and the true invasion was to take place elsewhere?'

'Elsewhere? Where?'

Karl signalled to the projectionist. An image of a long, sandy beach appeared on the screen. 'Two days ago, on this beach in Normandy, our troops captured British equipment that evidently belonged to a geologist.'

'A geologist?' Von Rundstedt was astonished. 'You captured him? Tortured him? Took his picture, at least?'

Karl ignored the questions and turned to the third photo.

'A compass-watch, topographical measurements, sand samples – he left everything there, probably when he was frightened by the approach of one of our patrols. But I'm sure that this geologist was not able to get back to England.'

The room fell silent. Von Rundstedt came up to the screen to look more closely at the equipment depicted on it. Everyone held his breath. Then von Rundstedt turned to Karl.

'What if your cubes and your geologist were themselves a desperate, last-minute attempt to make us think the landing would not take place near Calais?'

'A geologist was there, I'm convinced of that,' Karl replied.

'What never fails to amaze me about the SS,' von Rundstedt said, 'is that you never doubt anything. The next time, Colonel, come back with concrete, sand and a set of structures.'

The audience laughed uproariously. Von Rundstedt indicated that the meeting was over. The hyenas followed him out of the room, without even looking at Karl.

On the way back to Paris, Volker tried to reassure Karl. 'I'm sure that you scored some points all the same. But Marshal von Rundstedt will always hold you to a higher standard – you don't belong to the same world, you're not Prussian.'

Karl, who hadn't said a word since they left Saint-Germain-en-Laye, was keeping his eyes on the countryside rolling past. 'We're not at war with Prussia, so far as I know. Whatever I do, that old goat will never take me seriously.'

Volker was silent for a moment, as if meditating on what Karl had said, before whispering in his ear, 'You could try to go around the Marshal…'

'How would I do that?'

'By talking to someone who could make your case directly to the Führer, for example.'

Karl understood to whom Volker was alluding. 'Rommel?'

'You know how much he likes you.'

Karl remembered the telephone call he'd received from Rommel after his failed wedding ceremony. Rommel was the only person who'd had a friendly word for him.

'He'll listen to you,' Volker went on. 'And if you can convince him, he might even be able to arrange an interview for you in Berlin.'

New hope blossomed in Karl's mind. The car came into the place des Pyramides.

'We have to find this geologist,' Karl said, getting out of the car. 'Without him, we can't do anything. That's our priority, understand?'

'Yes Sir, Colonel!'

'Thanks for your support, Volker. I won't forget what you've done for me.'

Volker was almost too brilliant. Sooner or later, he was going to try to get a more prestigious post than that of aide-de-camp. Was he really as loyal as Karl thought? How could he know whether Volker was also playing a double game?

Karl was waiting for the lift and mulling over all these questions when he suddenly heard a familiar voice behind him.

'Excuse me, do you have a moment, Colonel?'

It was a boy hardly twenty years old, wearing a dark grey three-piece suit. He was nervously turning his cap in his hands.

Eddy.

'I thought that by coming here I couldn't miss you. This time, I think I've found a rare pearl, no kidding, you're going to love her, I'm sure.'

Karl grimaced. Eddy smelled of cheap eau de cologne.

'Not now, Eddy, I'm sorry.'

The lift came. The attendant opened the door to let Heindrich in. 'Good day, Colonel. Are you going to the fourth floor?'

'Yes, please.'

The attendant was about to close the door when Eddy slipped into the lift with them.

'Colonel, I've really put a lot of effort into this – it wasn't easy, you know.'

'If it were easy, my little friend, I'd do it myself.'

'At least come have a look for a minute, so that I'll know if I'm on the right track.'

Karl looked hard at him. He couldn't quite detest Eddy. The boy's tenacity pleased him. He'd also been aggressive once.

The lift stopped at the fourth floor. The attendant opened the door to let them out. But Karl didn't budge.

'Where is she?' he murmured to Eddy in an expressionless voice.

Smiling, the boy put his cap back on.

'In the usual place, Colonel.'

Karl left them and went down the stairs to the third floor. There, he took the corridor leading to the wing of the hotel where the rooms had not yet been requisitioned. When he arrived in front of the door to room 813, his heart beat faster. He couldn't help it, he always felt just as apprehensive every time he came back.

He turned the doorhandle. The door opened easily. His heart pounding, he went into the vestibule. The flowers had been changed, and Liliane's perfume floated in the air.

Perfect. So far, everything was going well.

He closed the door and started down the hallway. Passing in front of the bathroom, he saw that the light was on. The light distracted him. He'd asked that everything be just right. The first error. Irritated, he flipped the switch to turn off the light. His palms were moist. He continued, and finally entered the bedroom.

The woman was standing motionless in front of the window. Karl couldn't believe his eyes. The silhouette, the hair, the hat, the dress – everything was the same. But he hadn't yet seen her face. Generally, he was overcome by disappointment and bitterness at that point. Why take the risk, he thought.

'Don't turn around.' He'd spoken in a soft voice, but the girl stiffened nonetheless. Then he moved towards a table where he'd set up a record-player. He put the tone arm on the record, and music filled the room. The girl seemed more at ease now; she swayed her hips to the rhythm of the melody. Karl slowly came up to her, being careful not to look her in the face. He concentrated on her chignon, which was just like Liliane's, well above the neck, like a promise of happiness. He put his hands on her shoulders and closed his eyes. Her fragrance suddenly filled his nostrils, and images flooded into his mind. Liliane, in her dressing room, the day they first met. Liliane on horseback at Rambouillet, Liliane on top of him, in the bed behind them.

It was working.

He held her more tightly in his arms. She responded to him. He was ready. His eyes still closed, he whispered, 'Now.'

As she raised her veil it caressed his cheek. Her lips found his, sought his tongue, then pulled back in order to come back again, kissing furtively his chin and his neck. His excitement grew. The girl was now kissing him more uninhibitedly, her body pressed against his. Their tongues intertwined passionately, and he couldn't resist the desire to hold her face in his hands.

The same skin. Eddy hadn't lied. He'd found a rare pearl.

His eyes still closed, he felt the girl's lips leaving his. She had knelt down and was unbuttoning his trousers. She wanted him, and couldn't wait any longer. He frowned. Something was bothering him.

It was all going too fast.

He opened his eyes.

It wasn't Liliane.

He lifted her to her feet. She pulled him towards her and tried to kiss him again, but he pushed her against the window. Now he saw her clearly; her face was rounder than Liliane's, and her eyes were not the same colour. Without giving her another look, he turned on his heel and left the room. Breathless, Heindrich hurried into the stairway and headed for his office.

He really had to stop this nonsense, he had to forget Liliane. He had so much work to do, he couldn't waste any more time!

Mounting the stairs two at a time, Karl suddenly realized that tears were running down his cheeks. Shocked, he stopped and dried his eyes with his handkerchief. On the next floor, he could hear voices. He shuddered. No one must see him in such a state. No one must know. Finally, he calmed down, drew a deep breath, and went up the last few steps to the fourth floor.

Louise

After serving more than a fortnight in Section F, Louise was still spending most of her time typing correspondence. She wanted to escape from this dull, dreary life that didn't at all suit her. Pierre tried to be reassuring, telling her that Buckmaster hadn't forgotten her and that she should be patient. But she suspected her brother of using his influence to keep her from being assigned to a mission on the continent. Louise was also angry at Romans and Chabot for having sent her there, and was trying to find a way to contact them to negotiate her return.

Then one morning, at breakfast, Pierre said without even looking at her, 'Buck and I want to talk to you today.'

'What about? Isn't the correspondence typed the way you want it?'

'We have a problem, and it's rather urgent.'

Urgent: the word was well chosen. In his office, Buck didn't bother with preliminaries: 'How long were you a nurse in Nantua?'

Disappointed, Louise glanced at Pierre; had they brought her here to offer her a job as a nurse? 'I never really stopped.'

'Would you like to start nursing again?'

'I could continue to do that in France. I didn't come here to take care of the wounded.'

Buck gave Pierre a satisfied look. 'It would be more a matter of evacuating a wounded man. He's in a German hospital in Normandy.'

40

Pierre remained silent. Louise looked the colonel straight in the eye. He didn't seem to be joking.

'You want me to evacuate a wounded German?'

'He's an Englishman disguised as a German,' Pierre explained, opening his mouth for the first time.

'What is this crazy story? I'm not sure I understand.'

'That's what the poor fellow must have said to himself when he realized what was happening to him.'

Buck got up and paced back and forth in the office. Pierre took over.

'He's a geologist who's working for us. He was operating on the Normandy coast when a German saw him. He had to kill the man and put on his uniform in order to get away.'

Louise felt her interest reviving. 'That was pretty *culotté* of him.'

Buck suddenly stopped walking. He looked confused. '*Culotté*?'

'It means cheeky,' Pierre explained.

Although Buck spoke French, from time to time he got stuck on a word or expression. He started pacing up and down again. 'Cheeky... I'd say stupid. The British took him for a German and he was hit by RAF bombs near Lisieux.

'Naturally, the Germans took him to a Wehrmacht hospital in Pont-l'Évêque,' Pierre explained.

'What was your geologist doing on the coast of Normandy?' Louise asked.

'Something the Nazis mustn't under any circumstances find out about,' Pierre said.

Louise looked doubtful. She would have liked to know more, but Buck had already moved on to another subject.

'Have you heard of Colonel Karl Heindrich?'

Louise shook her head.

'For a long time, he worked in counter-espionage. Recently he was named head of the SS's intelligence services.'

'He's already trying to track down our geologist,' Pierre added, glancing at his sister.

Louise looked impassive, but her mind was racing. 'Do you really think I could get your guy out of that hornets' nest, all by myself, disguised as a nurse?'

'You won't be alone,' the colonel replied. 'There will be five women in all, under Pierre's command, and they'll be there with you. One of our agents who's already in France, an Italian woman whose code name is Maria, will meet you. For the rest of the team, Pierre and I have found recruits who can help you. Some have already been trained as commandos…'

He handed her a file containing information on several women, along with their photos. Louise noticed that a few of the photos had been taken from police records.

'Some of them are in prison?'

'Yes, they'll be pardoned if the mission is successful.'

'How long do you think training will take?'

'Two days to bring you up to date. You'll be sent out on the evening of the second day.'

'Two days? Are you serious?'

'Time is short, Louise.'

'Time is short? I've been wasting my time here for two weeks filing documents that no one cares about and letters that no one reads, so don't tell me that!'

Buck was piqued, and immediately reacted. 'Our geologist disappeared three days ago. The mission was decided upon yesterday.

It has to be Monday. If you don't want to go, I have some correspondence here that needs filing.'

Louise lowered her eyes. Pierre shot Buck a look that said, 'I told you so.'

'If you're interested, I'm ready to answer your questions.'

'You said there'd be five of us. Isn't that a lot of nurses?'

'Only you and Maria will be nurses.'

'Ah? So what will the others be doing meanwhile?'

Buck turned to Pierre. 'Pierre will explain it to you in greater detail. Unfortunately, I have to leave you because I have an urgent meeting in ten minutes. I'm glad that you've accepted this assignment, Louise. I'll see you very soon.'

He hurried out of the office. Louise couldn't help thinking that he was escaping and leaving her brother to do the dirty work.

'So? What are the others supposed to do?' she asked, apparently imperturbable.

Pierre cleared his throat, then started describing the mission in detail. At first, Louise thought it was a joke. When she realized that her brother was serious, she got very annoyed. Pierre let her shout; he didn't want to get involved, and besides, he had no argument with her. Down deep, he knew she wasn't completely wrong.

Half an hour later, sitting across from Pierre in the mess hall, Louise was still angry. Buck was sitting a few tables away, eating lunch with some officers, and seemed a little embarrassed. Louise looked at him furiously as she devoured her fish and chips without even tasting them.

'That's really the stupidest idea I've heard in a long time. How many of you did it take to come up with it?'

'Just Buck and me.'

'It sounds more like you.'

'It's the only way of getting him out of there, believe me; we've considered every possibility.'

'Did you also consider just sending us directly to be slaughtered?'

'If we don't do something, several thousand men will be on their way to being slaughtered, as you put it.'

Louise calmed down. She took a bite of fish and glanced at the colonel, who was still gazing down at his plate. 'The mission is connected with the invasion, isn't it?'

Pierre didn't answer, but she knew him well enough to realize what his silence meant. She was no longer angry, though she still found their idea stupid.

'The first candidate is waiting for us, and it would be better not to be late.'

'Why?'

'She's supposed to be hanged at two p.m. We have to pick up a letter at the Home Office beforehand, otherwise it will be impossible to stop the execution.' Louise put her cutlery on her plate and drained a glass of water.

'Let's go!'

Rain was pouring on Luton Prison. In the courtyard, a scaffold had been erected. At its foot, the hangman was waiting, his arms crossed, accompanied by a clergyman and a thirty-year-old woman. The woman's hands and feet were in chains, and she was beginning to show signs of impatience.

'Well, what's going on now? Why aren't you getting on with it? Who are those two, there?' Further on, standing under an umbrella, the directress of the prison was negotiating with Pierre and Louise, who were soaked to the skin.

'I don't understand why the execution has been cancelled. This woman is an irredeemable murderess.'

'The file is classified, Madam, I can't tell you any more than that.'

She read through once more the letter Pierre and Louise had brought her, slipped it into her pocket with a resigned air, and announced that the execution had been cancelled. The condemned woman was at first speechless.

'Well, how about that? You never know when you're going to get good news.'

A few minutes later, Pierre and Louise joined her in her cell.

'Jeanne Faussier? We'd like to talk with you. My name is Pierre Desfontaines, and this is Louise Granville.'

Louise felt a slight tremor. For the first time, her brother had called her by her married name. She was touched. Jeanne looked them over as she finished changing her clothes.

'So, it's to you that I owe my continued existence. Are you sure you haven't made a mistake? Because I did kill somebody, you know.'

'Your pimp – I wouldn't call him "somebody",' Louise retorted.

Jeanne smiled at her. 'Nobody ever made me do anything I didn't want to do, sweetie!'

'Precisely,' Pierre said. 'If you reject our proposal, the execution might well be merely postponed.'

'Ah, so that's it. I knew there'd be a catch,' Jeanne said, disgusted. 'What do you want?'

Louise took over. 'We need you for a mission in France. A dangerous mission.'

'In France, huh? I've got to fuck somebody, I suppose. Who? Pétain? I warn you, I never do old men, that's always made me sick.'

'According to our information, you were a nude dancer in a Soho cabaret,' Pierre said.

Jeanne laughed. 'I don't believe this! You need a girl who can dance?'

'Answer the question.'

'Yeah, I did that, sure, and I've done a lot of other things, too, but if you've come looking for me somebody must have really put a knife to your throat.'

Pierre looked at his sister. He was almost ready to explode.

'We also need a girl who can kill,' said Louise, still deadpan.

'What's in it for me, apart from not getting bumped off today?'

For Pierre she had now gone too far. 'Really, where do you think you are? Do you think you're in a position to set conditions now?'

'Pierre, calm down. Excuse him,' Louise said to Jeanne, 'he's a little on edge.'

'It's okay, I know how that is,' Jeanne replied. 'But to tell you the truth, I don't trust all this, it doesn't feel right. But thanks for thinking of me.' She called out to the guards. 'Call the directress, we're going back!'

Louise was surprised to find herself grabbing Jeanne's arm. 'You're going to die like a whore who never had a choice, is that really what you want? I'm asking you to choose. With me, you can go out without regretting anything, and you might come back with your head held high. If the mission succeeds, you'll not only be pardoned, you'll even get a medal.'

These words, which had come out spontaneously, moved Jeanne. 'At least you know how to talk to women.'

Exasperated, Pierre looked up at the ceiling. For the first time in ages, Louise found herself smiling.

A few hours later, Pierre and Louise were sitting comfortably in Berlemont's, a London pub where Pierre often went, and which was frequented by many officers in the SOE and the Free French forces. He had arranged to meet their next candidate there, a woman named Gaëlle Lemenech. But he was still annoyed with Jeanne, and even more with Louise.

'She's a complete psychopath. We'll never be able to trust her, don't you understand? She's a madwoman, didn't you see that? Why did you insist?'

'She had the rope around her neck and she turned us down. I don't know many people who would've had the guts, not even crazies. I'd prefer to speak to the next candidate myself, if you don't mind.'

Pierre stared defiantly at her, then leapt to his feet, his beer in his hand.

'What? Where are you going?'

'I'm going to let you handle this one all by yourself, just to see, because I don't know how to talk to women.'

'That's not what I meant.'

But Pierre had already gone to join his fellow officers, who were standing at the bar and welcomed him with open arms. Sighing,

Louise saw several of them who were pretty tipsy pointing to her and making remarks to her brother, whose implication was not difficult to decipher. She also saw him shaking his head and forming the words 'She's my sister' with his lips. But this did not stop the remarks; on the contrary. A giant well over six feet tall came over to ask her to join them. She declined politely, giving a professional appointment as her excuse. Disappointed, the giant handed her his card and invited her to have a drink some time when she was less busy. In very imperfect French he added, 'Hurry, because I might be dead tomorrow.'

Louise didn't know how to respond. The man smiled at her and then went back to the bar, where he exchanged a few words with Pierre, who found it all quite amusing. Louise looked at the name on the card: John Forbes. She liked him, and appreciated his not having pushed too hard. Would she call him some time? She hadn't the slightest idea.

Since Claude's death, she hadn't paid special attention to any man, even for a moment, and she hadn't accepted any invitations. Nonetheless, on the ship that carried her to England, and in the streets of London, there had been no lack of opportunities. She seemed no longer to feel any desire. It was as if her body were anesthetized. She remembered the last time she'd made love with Claude at the Morez farm, the day before the operation in Bourg-en-Bresse. Fanfan and the others had gone out to reconnoitre, and Louise and Claude, finally alone, had glanced at each other with the same love and yearning. They hadn't had many chances to show the desire that they felt for one another, and if the mission should go badly they would at least take with them this memory. Even though Louise had slept with many men before her husband, she'd never felt any particular physical revelation. But on that morning in Morez, despite the tension, despite the fatigue, Louise had felt so deeply excited that she'd told Claude that she wanted to feel him inside her, right away. The intense, indescribable emotion that overcame her had ultimately left her weak and saddened. For if she died the next day, she would never relive the intimate and unsuspected pleasure that she had discovered so late in her life.

'Are you the person I'm supposed to meet?'

Immersed in her memories, Louise had not noticed the young woman who was speaking to her.

'I'm Gaëlle Lemenech.'

'I'm sorry, I was elsewhere. How do you do? I'm Louise Granville.' Louise invited Gaëlle to sit down. They shook hands, and the young woman, who couldn't have been more than twenty-one, surprised her with the strength of her grip. Louise admired the energy that radiated from her.

'Excuse me for being late, but it's the General's fault; he let us go only a little while ago.'

A Free French corporal came up to their table to greet Gaëlle. 'Hello, Binette, how are you getting along?'

'As best I can, Pioche, take care of yourself.'

Louise frowned. '"Hoe"? "Shovel"?'

'Excuse us, it's a custom in our section of the Free French. We all use the names of tools; at first they called me 'Rake', but I found that nickname a bit of a loser. I didn't want it to bring me bad luck. I did the right thing, don't you think?'

Amused, Louise gave in. Gaëlle had been there for less than a minute, and she liked her already. The young woman looked hungry, and was trying to find the waiter. Her eyes met Pierre's; he was still watching Louise from the bar, a smile on his lips. A waiter came to take their order.

'What would you like, Miss?'

'I'll have leeks in vinaigrette, steak with chips, a baba au rhum, a beer, and coffee, black.'

Louise noticed a thin gold chain around Gaëlle's neck, from which hung a gilt cross. The woman was both a scientist and a believer – she obviously wasn't bothered by any paradox, and Louise liked that too. 'What are you doing at de Gaulle's offices, apart from training saboteurs? Have you already sent some of them on missions in France?'

'No, and that's my only regret,' Gaëlle replied. 'Making bombs without exploding them gets a little frustrating – it's like doing half the job.'

'With me, you'll be able to go all the way. I'm asking you to go to France.'

Gaëlle looked stunned. At that moment, the waiter brought her leeks in vinaigrette. She unfolded her napkin and, without waiting, attacked her meal. 'Excuse me,' she said, 'I'm starting because I'm starving.'

'Answer me all the same and you'll be excused everything.'

'I'd love to go back to France, but I'm sorry, I can't. My boss is de Gaulle, not Churchill. It's a matter of principle.'

Louise stared at her. 'Principle? But after all, if you knew that I was with the SOE, why did you come?'

Gaëlle gave her an innocent look. 'Because I never refuse a dinner invitation.'

Louise knew that this was the woman she needed. Her service reports described her as the best explosives expert in London, capable of building a bomb out of practically nothing at all. She wasn't going to let her get away that easily.

While Gaëlle was finishing her leeks, she noticed Pierre stealing furtive glances at Louise from the bar. 'Would you allow me, Louise?' Gaëlle asked.

'What?'

Gaëlle leaned towards her and whispered, 'I think that officer over there is seriously interested in you.'

'Who's that?'

'The lieutenant at the bar, the one who's smoking. If I were you, I wouldn't hesitate. Tomorrow, we might all be dead.'

Louise was astonished. Around here they all had the same phrase on their lips. She turned to look at Pierre, who gave her a big smile.

Gaëlle stared at him. 'Good lord, what a smile he has! Do you see how irresistible he is?' That gave Louise an idea. She asked Gaëlle to excuse her a moment and moved over to the bar. Gaëlle saw her talking with the handsome lieutenant. From where she sat, she couldn't hear what they were saying, but soon she saw the young man's face tense. Obviously he didn't appreciate the way Louise had approached him.

Pierre was having trouble controlling himself. 'Do you realize what you're asking me to do?'

'It's the only way, I sense it. I might be mistaken, but at least then we'd have tried everything.'

'Why are you stuck on that one? You'd think she's a little girl, just look at her!'

'That little girl is an outstanding chemist, she speaks German perfectly, and she was at the top of her commando class.'

Pierre paused. He watched Gaëlle devouring her steak and chips. She gave him a big smile. 'All the same, it's humiliating,' he said, stubbing out his cigarette.

'I've known you to be less finicky.'

Without saying anything more, Pierre went up to Gaëlle. A few minutes later they left the restaurant together.

The drawing room clock struck ten. It sounded like the one in Le Bérail, Louise thought. She suspected her brother of having chosen this clock because it reminded him of the family château. A detail like that summed up Pierre's personality; his motto might have been 'Move forward without ever forgetting tradition', whereas Louise's had more to do with scorched earth policies. In that respect, she was in perfect accord with the image of the SOE. Churchill had said that he created it to 'set Europe ablaze'. Louise's eyes were burning. She realized now that she'd been reading for several hours by the dim light of her bedside lamp. Stretched out on the sofa, with the files given her by Buck piled around her on the cushions, she'd spent the evening going over the profiles of the candidates Section F had proposed. Buck had personally written her to recommend one of them, a disguised way of forcing her hand.

Louise gazed at the photo of the woman in question. Suzy Verdier, twenty-seven, currently working at the First Aid Nursing Yeomanry, a volunteer service commonly known by its acronym,

FANY. Now that Louise understood all the aspects of the mission, she could see that Suzy's exceptional beauty was an undeniable advantage for their mission. On the other hand, the photos accompanying her file revealed another side of her personality. In a snapshot dated 28 February 1942, she was posing, in a dress with a plunging neckline, on the arm of a Nazi officer at an evening party in Paris. In another, she wore the costume of the mistress of ceremonies at a revue, and was inviting the same officer to join her on stage. A file of supplementary information revealed that Suzy's real name was Liliane Rosay. It also indicated that she had suddenly left France two years earlier, for unknown reasons. Why was the colonel advising them to include in the operation the former mistress of a German officer?

A vehicle stopped in front of the house. Louise looked up and saw her brother getting out of the car, looking completely dazed. She'd not been expecting him so soon, and wondered whether something had gone wrong with Gaëlle. When Pierre came in, she took one glance at him and told herself that all was lost. But Pierre closed the door and said simply, 'It's okay, she'll be coming along.'

Louise felt herself relax. Pierre took off his jacket and hung it on a coatstand that also reminded her of Le Bérail.

'It wasn't too difficult?' She regretted asking the question that way, but he didn't seem to take offence.

'Listening to her talk about Scouting in Quimper, her fiancé doing forced labour in Germany, the strength Jesus gives her, that was hard. I didn't stay because she could've gone on like that all night.'

'She wasn't offended? That you didn't stay?'

'Because I should've stayed? She accepted – isn't that enough for you?' Without saying another word, he walked across the room and went into the bedroom, closing the door behind him.

Pierre

Why had he agreed to put Louise up at his house? Slowly but surely, she was reasserting her grip on him. Pierre still hadn't got over the episode in Luton. Going on a mission with the psychopathic whore made no sense, and he feared that it was a major error. Should he speak to Buck about it? No, he had to resolve his problems by himself, as he'd done when he left Le Bérail.

With Gaëlle, too, he had to set things straight, because he'd behaved ignobly. Why had he told her, on the very first evening, about his desire to get married and have children? Why had he dangled before her the idea that she might be the woman he'd been waiting for? There was nothing less true, nothing more alien to his concerns. She'd believed him, with his air of having 'cradle-snatched', and that had increased his scorn and his pleasure in manipulating her. He'd enjoyed seeing her taken in by his biggest lies. Dominated by his sister, he was being sadistic towards an innocent girl. In other words, it was Louise's fault if he'd acted badly, despite himself. His sister always brought out the worst in him.

Pierre turned all this over in his mind as he drove to the FANY headquarters in Westminster. Sitting beside him, Louise continued reading over the file on their next candidate, Suzy.

'Why did Buckmaster recommend this girl – do you have any idea?' Louise asked.

Pierre put on an innocent smile. Buck had been very explicit: Louise didn't need to know everything. So he wasn't going to tell her any more than necessary. 'It seems she's an artiste, a pure one, and that's good, isn't it?'

'A dancer who fled France under a false name – you call that a pure artiste, do you?' Louise retorted.

'She danced at the Folies Bergère. Your whore in Luton can't say that much. And then she's rather pretty, don't you think?'

'Yes, maybe she's one of his old mistresses.'

'Buck's? Why do you say that?'

'She was sleeping with the Germans in France, why shouldn't she sleep with the English in Britain?'

'I find it hard to imagine Buck sending us one of his ex-mistresses to risk her life on a mission.'

'You do? You're sending your sister, aren't you?'

Pierre felt the blow. She was provoking him once again. He mustn't get upset. 'You're the one who wanted to leave, I remind you.'

'I know, I was just teasing you.'

She looked at him more tenderly. He had to be wary now.

The FANY was a group of civilian volunteers whose members were all involved in the war effort in very different ways. They drove ambulances, ran field hospitals, handled radio transmissions or deciphered codes. Some of them had also been parachuted into France by the SOE and hadn't come back. Suzy hadn't done anything like that. Since she'd arrived in Westminster, she'd had a redundant office job that left her a great deal of free time. Having endured the disappointments of enforced idleness herself, Louise felt an immediate empathy with Suzy. But Suzy didn't complain about her fate.

She was extraordinarily beautiful. The photographs were powerless to represent the peculiar luminosity that emanated from her skin and her eyes. Although she wore a forage cap and uniform of poor-quality fabric, Suzy was an almost celestial apparition. But this angel was not a saint, as her file clearly showed. The sound of her voice also stupefied them. Pierre and Louise felt the unreal spell that her arrival had cast break when she opened her mouth.

'It's not possible, I can't believe it!' Suzy squealed. She was looking at the two paris-brest pastries that Pierre had just unwrapped in front of her. 'They're my favourite! How did you know? Are you psychic, or what?'

'We're just well informed,' Pierre explained. She shivered. The tone of her voice changed. She was now on her guard.

'Informed about what? And why?'

'A pretty woman who never gains an ounce no matter how much she eats, you have to admit that that's intriguing, no?' Louise replied. 'Especially if she's been living in London for more than a year under a false identity…'

'Besides, Liliane is a nice name, and I wonder whether it doesn't still suit you better?' Pierre added, driving the point home.

Suzy recoiled. She looked like an animal about to spring. Louise put Suzy's file on the desk.

'Investigation has revealed that you were the mistress of a German officer at the time you were dancing at the Folies Bergère in 1942. For that reason alone, you could be shot.'

'We found the marriage bans,' Pierre added. 'But the wedding was never performed. Why?'

'Get up and take off that uniform. You've no right to wear it,' Louise said.

Suzy surged to her feet and started towards the door. Pierre stopped her and pinned her to the wall. Louise tried to hold him back, but he kept her at a distance. 'Let me deal with this one.'

He could feel Suzy's imprisoned body tremble like an insect impaled on a pin. Looking into her eyes, he was surprised to feel the same pleasure he'd felt with Gaëlle, and all the more because this time Louise was observing him. Suddenly ashamed of his behaviour, he loosened his grip.

'Why did you leave me alone until now if you knew all that?' Suzy mumbled.

'Because it's only now that we need you.'

'To do what?'

'To take a little forty-eight hour trip to the mother country, for the good cause, and you're not going to make us beg you…'

'I'll never return to France! I broke with my past, I broke my engagement, isn't that enough for you?'

'It's either that or face a military tribunal. You choose.'

Suzy nodded, then sank to the floor, hiding her face in her hands. Pierre ran his hand through his hair and turned towards Louise, who shot him a dark look. She detested him for having humiliated Suzy that way, and he knew it, but now he felt better. He'd re-established the balance of power.

The following morning, a bus came to pick up Pierre and Louise at 64 Baker Street. Gaëlle, Jeanne and Suzy were already on board, each of them sitting at a distance from the others. Suzy had placed herself as far as she could from Gaëlle and Jeanne. When she saw Pierre get on, Gaëlle stood up, radiant, but he ignored her and went to sit at the back of the bus. Louise chose to stay near the front. The bus started up again. Jeanne waited a few seconds before asking, 'Can you tell us where we're going?'

Louise saw no reason to hide their destination from her. 'To an SOE training camp at Beaulieu, in the New Forest.'

'And what are we going to do there, play soldiers?'

'You might say that, yes.'

'We still don't know what we're going to do in France.'

'You'll know soon enough, don't worry.'

'That fellow there, is it true he's your brother?'

From where he was sitting, Pierre could see his sister talking with the prisoner from Luton. By the furtive glances the latter gave him, he guessed that they were talking about him. Jeanne must be asking whether he had to be there, and Louise, though she thought he did not, was saying that he did. He sensed that Gaëlle was continuing to observe him with the worried air that women have when they realize that they've been lied to. What could she do? Suddenly jump up and demand that the bus stop, calling him a lout? That sort of thing didn't correspond with her temperament, and he thought she wouldn't cause any problems. Nonetheless, she would certainly confront him at Beaulieu. How would he react? Just thinking about it tied his stomach in knots, and he wanted to get away. At times like that, he envied his sister's detachment, the coolness she displayed in the most dramatic situations. Between feeling and duty, she always chose without hesitation. He was still incapable of doing that. He was definitely not good at playing the tough guy.

Despite their disagreements, Pierre thought Louise was right in saying that this training at Beaulieu was like an operetta rehearsal. In two days, what could they teach girls who for the most part had never held a weapon or used a parachute? Technically, not much, that was sure. But throwing them into the deep end without even having given them a moment to get to know each other better would have been even more suicidal. Pierre was well aware that the mission's success depended in large measure on Suzy and Jeanne. However, no one had yet told them what their role would be, and he feared their reaction. What would they do if they proved incapable of carrying out the task assigned to them? He was not worried about Suzy, who was very professional, but Jeanne's unpredictable nature filled him with dread. Another aspect of the mission alarmed him as well: Buck's choice of Suzy was no accident. Even if Louise suspected something, Pierre was the only one who knew that the operation would have a second act.

The bus's advance was slowed by roadworks. Jeanne began to find the trip long. She turned to Gaëlle, who was seated behind her. 'We haven't been introduced. What's your name?'

'Gaëlle Lemenech.'

'I'm Jeanne. Where do you come from, Gaëlle?'

'From Quimper. You?'

'I'm from Burgundy, but you wouldn't know the name of the village, it's too small and remote. Fortunately for me, I left there early on. What were you doing in Quimper? Were you on the game too?'

Seeing Gaëlle's alarm, Louise signalled her to remain calm.

'No, I was a chemist.'

Jeanne looked at Gaëlle sceptically, as if she had replied in a foreign tongue. She didn't inquire further; instead she moved closer to Suzy, who had been more standoffish from the outset. 'Hello, my name is Jeanne. What's yours?'

On her guard, Suzy hesitated before shaking Jeanne's hand. 'Suzy. Pleased to meet you.'

'Where do you come from, Suzy, and what did you do before?' Jeanne asked, using the familiar *tu*.

59

'I don't like to be addressed *tu*, I can tell you that right now.'

'Oh! Easy, honey, we're all in the same boat. What makes you think you're any better than me anyway? Who have you bumped off? Come on, let's compare – in my case, it was my pimp. How about you?'

Suzy was struck dumb. Pierre had a feeling she was going to break down and sob.

'Well?' Jeanne was impatient.

'Leave her alone,' Pierre shouted. 'Can't you see you're upsetting her?'

Jeanne sighed and went back to her seat. 'Three days of this is going to be fun,' she grumbled. For the rest of the trip, no one spoke a word.

The Beaulieu training camp was in the heart of Hampshire, on the land of the Montagu family, who had a stately home there. When they arrived just before noon, the women were pleasantly surprised by the setting, which was not very military. They were quickly disillusioned when they were introduced to the instructor charged with teaching them how to use weapons and jump out of a plane with a parachute.

To Pierre's great surprise, Gaëlle did not confront him. She didn't meet his eyes even once in the refectory or during lessons. His interest in her, which was then at its low point, was oddly revived.

A mock-up of the military hospital that they were supposed to get into had been set up in the large drawing room, following information provided by Maria, who was already there. The team sat around the model, Pierre took charge and presented the mission.

'In Le Havre, there's a cabaret, La Femme et la Bière, that special-izes in dance numbers. Three days from now, at the request of the director of the hospital, a show will be given at the hospital to amuse the patients. While Louise and Maria infiltrate the place disguised as nurses, the others will come on aboard the cabaret's vehicle, which they will intercept en route. Jeanne and Suzy will take the place of the dancers, Gaëlle will take the place of the dresser, and I'll take the place of the driver. There'll be two other men with us.'

Then Pierre explained exactly what each person's role would be. He told Gaëlle which vehicles she was to blow up, Louise which room the geologist was in. He quickly arrived at Suzy's and Jeanne's roles. 'While Louise and Maria are on the second floor evacuating the wounded man, Suzy and Jeanne will keep the Germans busy by doing their number on stage.'

Jeanne frowned. 'Our number? What's that?'

'You're going to do a dance number so spectacular that it will attract all the armed men in the hospital.'

'With her?' Jeanne asked, pointing at Suzy. 'She didn't even want to tell me where she came from, so don't imagine that she's going to dance with me, honey.'

'That's enough, no need to go on about it,' Suzy protested.

'How long is it supposed to last, this dance number?' Jeanne asked.

'About twenty minutes. The exact length will be determined down to the second.'

'And you want all the men in the hospital looking at us for twenty minutes? What do you think you're going to get us to do?'

'A strip-tease,' Pierre confessed, almost ashamed.

No one said anything for a moment. Louise lowered her eyes. Gaëlle's mouth remained open, like Suzy's, whereas Jeanne exploded with laughter. 'Is that your brilliant idea?'

Suzy reacted. 'That will never work. They won't last for twenty minutes, and neither will we. I know what I'm talking about; I started out doing strip-teases, and I can tell you that even ten minutes is long.'

'You won't be just taking off your clothes,' Pierre went on. 'We've hired a trainer who will explain everything to you, and will work with you for as long as it takes.' He opened a door, and a woman of about fifty came in. Unlike the other agents, she was not in uniform, and was the very image of what Jeanne would look like in thirty years. 'This is Mrs Lynn.'

Without even looking around, the woman went directly up to Suzy and Jeanne, examining them from head to foot as if they were livestock. Apparently satisfied, she gestured to them to follow her. Jeanne and Suzy remained seated, not feeling inclined to obey.

'Has this old bat ever heard of manners? Who does she think we are? We're not pieces of meat.'

Mrs Lynn started shouting so loudly that Suzy almost fell over backwards: 'Move your fucking arse!'

Pierre looked at his sister, who seemed terribly embarrassed. Shaken, Jeanne and Suzy left the room with the creature, who slammed the door behind her. In a room upstairs, they began rehearsing to music.

After a few minutes, Suzy came back, half weeping. 'I can't do that, I'm an artiste, a professional, what you're asking me to do is vile!'

Louise couldn't have agreed more, but she gritted her teeth. To Pierre's great surprise, it was Jeanne who came to look for Suzy. 'Come on, it's going to be all right, you'll see, you've got to trust me,' she said to her.

'How do you expect me to trust her? That woman is a murderess!' Suzy cried desperately.

Then Mrs Lynn appeared. She was very threatening, and reduced Suzy to the point of complete breakdown. Louise looked away, disgusted. Jeanne remained unmoved, evidently wounded by Suzy's remark. Mrs Lynn took the weeping Suzy by the arm and led her back to the practice room, where the music went on until evening. Pierre told himself that his worst fears had just been confirmed.

During the evening an incident occurred that almost compromised everything. The house provided lockers where new recruits could store their personal effects. Louise put her things in her locker, along with the files on Suzy, Jeanne and Gaëlle. When she turned the key in the lock, it broke off. She went to the dormitory to look for the maintenance man. Jeanne, who had just come out of the shower, saw Louise's locker open. After checking that no one was watching her, she glanced inside it and saw Suzy's file, which she began going through eagerly. Although she had trouble deciphering the dozens of pages typed in English, she could easily understand the photos showing a young woman drinking toasts with numerous German officers. Determined, she put the file back in its place and dressed, as though nothing had happened.

A welcome bar had been set up in one of the estate's outbuildings. Agents and instructors generally met there for a drink after a day of training. When Pierre and Louise entered the room, the first thing they saw was Suzy sitting on the lap of the soldier who was playing the piano. Seeing the light in her eyes, Louise immediately understood that Suzy was completely drunk. Suzy glanced at her, and maliciously whispered a few words to the pianist, who started playing the first notes of 'Douce France'. But the words Suzy sang were not the familiar ones: 'Lousy France, I don't give a damn about your suffering, seeing your tongue hanging out, under the occupiers' yoke.' Pierre started towards her. Louise stopped him dead. At the same moment, Jeanne and Gaëlle appeared. Suzy continued to sing: 'My village, with its church tower, its modest houses, where children my age are now whores or collaborators … I hate you, in resentment and pain, lousy France, I don't give a damn about your suffering, seeing you with your tongue hanging out, under the occupiers' yoke.' The British soldiers, who hadn't understood the words, applauded wildly. Suzy bowed to her audience before downing another glass of rum.

Louise, who had joined her at the bar, snapped at her, 'All right, are you proud of yourself? Have you produced your little effect?'

'What? Don't we still have the right to relax?'

'Relax, yes, show off in such a deplorable way, no.'

'You want me to tell you what's deplorable? It's forcing me to go back to that shitty country that has never done anything for me!'

'If I had the choice, I'd refuse to take you with me. You should be ashamed of yourself.'

'Shame – she's covered in it, where she is…' Jeanne had come up treacherously to challenge Suzy. 'Once you've fucked Boches, you're not likely to blush at anything. But she gets sensitive when she has to dance a little too close to me – poor girl!'

Suzy turned ninety degrees. 'A whore talking to me about shame, I can't believe this!' she screamed in Jeanne's face.

'I prefer being a whore to being a collabo.'

Suzy raised her hand to slap her, but Jeanne stopped her.

'Do you know what I do to tarts like you?' With one hand, Jeanne took Suzy by the throat, with the other she pressed a knife against her cheek. Louise intervened before the blade could cut Suzy's flesh. The knife slid to the ground. Suddenly one could have heard a pin drop. Pierre gave Jeanne a slap so hard that she tumbled to the floor. Gaëlle tried to help her get up, but Jeanne pushed her away.

'If you ever touch me again, you bastard, I'll kill you all. You don't know what I'm capable of!' She left the mess hall without looking at Suzy. Gaëlle followed her. Louise led Suzy away to sleep in the dormitory. Pierre remained alone, plunged in deep despair. Should he inform the colonel this evening, or wait until tomorrow? He ordered a glass of whisky and tried to decide what to do. Through the window, he saw Gaëlle talking to Jeanne, without hearing a word of what they were saying. To his considerable stupefaction, Jeanne started crying. Gaëlle took her in her arms and they remained like that for a long time. Then they both came back into the barracks.

Several minutes went by, and Pierre was starting on his third glass of whisky when Louise came in. 'What happened?' she asked. Pierre turned towards her, not knowing how to tell her that he'd decided to get drunk. But Louise hadn't come to talk to him about his drunkenness. 'Was it you who spoke to Jeanne?' she continued. It took Pierre a moment to understand.

'Spoke about what?'

'She came to the dormitory to say she was sorry; she was crying like a baby and begging Suzy to forgive her. When I left them they were hugging each other.'

Pierre looked at his half-full glass and set it back on the bar. 'I didn't say anything to her. It was Gaëlle who talked to her.'

'Gaëlle? Where is she?'

Pierre shrugged. A corporal reported that he'd seen the young woman going into the chapel behind the castle. The members of the Montagu family were the only ones who went there, but it remained open day and night, available to anyone who wanted to meditate. It was there that they found Gaëlle, kneeling on a prie-dieu. Pierre remembered the evening they had spent together and the emphasis the young woman put on religion in her life. For his sister and himself, religious faith was nothing more than the memory of their father, to the point that they forgot that a member of the Resistance could be a believer. Since the war started, Louise had refused to enter a church, and her marriage to Claude, who was an atheist, had radicalized her position.

'I can't go in there,' Louise said. 'But you can; try to find out what she said to Jeanne.' She turned on her heel and left.

Pierre went to sit down on a bench next to Gaëlle, who had closed her eyes. She sensed his presence, but didn't move. 'I saw you talking with Jeanne a little while ago,' Pierre said. 'What did you say to her?'

It was the first time Pierre had spoken to Gaëlle since the evening they had spent together. Gaëlle remained silent, with her eyes closed. He was about to get up and leave when she answered him. 'I tried to explain to her that hatred doesn't make things better, and that faith can save you. I think she understood, in her own way.' Confused and embarrassed, Pierre just nodded. Gaëlle left the chapel, leaving Pierre alone on the bench, speechless. He would never again judge someone on a first impression.

The following day began with parachute jumps from the hot-air balloon anchored on the castle lawn. To everyone's great relief, no accidents slowed the test. All the women executed jumps so perfect as to give the impression that Gaëlle's prayers had won them all grace. Jeanne and Suzy retained no trace of enmity. Louise ended up being the most ill-humoured, not saying a word to anyone all morning. Pierre tried to sound her out, but she just said she'd passed a sleepless night; he didn't insist. The rehearsals of Suzy and Jeanne's dance number continued behind closed doors. Nonetheless, Mrs Lynn persisted in shouting her commands, which could be heard even in the mess hall. Then it was time to give the agents the new names they would use for the duration of the assignment. Pierre handed out passes, ration cards and other identity papers. He asked the women to memorize them in every detail. Jeanne was not happy when she saw her new name.

'Do you think I look like a Raymonde? For a music-hall artiste, that's not so great, no?'

Pierre ignored her remark and continued his explanations. 'If the Gestapo arrests you, the order is not to say anything for forty-eight hours.'

'Why forty-eight?' Suzy asked.

'That's how long the other members of the team will need to take cover.'

'What if they torture us?'

'If you speak too soon, you'll be sacrificing the others,' Pierre said. 'As a last resort, you'll have this.' He showed them a small white pill. Gaëlle did not conceal her uneasiness.

'Is that cyanide?'

'Keep it well hidden,' Pierre went on, handing out the pills. 'If you need to, swallow it. The poison takes effect in a few seconds.'

'And then, bye-bye Raymonde!' Jeanne said, contemplating her pill absently.

The plane was to take off at dawn from the military airfield at Tempsford, a few kilometres from Beaulieu. They spent the final hours before departure preparing their packs and camouflaging their faces. Gaëlle wanted to go back to the chapel to pray, but she didn't have time. At six p.m. they boarded a vehicle that deposited them a quarter of an hour later on the tarmac at the airfield. Pierre and Buck were already waiting for them there. The colonel gave Louise a valise full of French money to cover 'unforeseen expenses'. Each woman received a bundle of notes. Seeing the other notes lined up in the valise, Jeanne couldn't help asking, 'How much is in there?'

'Enough,' Louise answered, closing the valise.

Buck wished them all good luck, and then a clergyman blessed the plane, a Whitley bomber, as well as each of the passengers about to board it.

'Have you ever been blessed before?' Suzy asked Jeanne apprehensively.

'Me? When I get down on my knees it's not usually to pray, if you want to know the truth.'

Just before she climbed into the fuselage, Gaëlle discreetly threw away her cyanide pill. Louise, who was just behind her, picked it up and then went to join Gaëlle at the back of the plane. She handed her the pill. 'You dropped this, I think.'

Gaëlle remained calm. 'Suicide is contrary to my religion,' she said.

'God doesn't give a damn about our affairs.'

'Are you saying that because of your husband?'

Louise stiffened. How could Gaëlle have known about that? She glanced at Pierre, who had been watching them and had heard everything. He felt uncomfortable.

'My brother was shot on his twentieth birthday,' Gaëlle went on. 'That doesn't keep me from believing.'

'That's your problem.'

Gaëlle did not hear Louise's answer because the deafening roar of the engines suddenly drowned it out. The plane sped down the runway and rose slowly into the air. Through a porthole, Pierre saw Buck's silhouette moving away over the tarmac before disappearing into the landscape. They were on their way.

No one said a word as they crossed the Channel. As they approached the French coast, they heard the pilot's voice: 'Hang on, we're going to climb!'

'That's to escape the German anti-aircraft batteries,' Pierre explained. 'We're going in over France.' The bomber gained altitude. The women were abruptly thrown backwards. Their faces tense, they held on as best they could to the metal frameworks of their seats. New sounds soon competed with the roar of the engines, accompanied by flashes of light outside the portholes. The plane shook violently several times, and the women began to scream.

Suzy leapt to her feet. 'We can't jump. They're shooting at us! They'll shoot us down like rabbits!' Without allowing her to say more, Louise coldly slapped her. Pierre and Gaëlle forced Suzy to sit down again, and Jeanne took her hand. Suzy closed her eyes and bit her lip. Alongside her Gaëlle was murmuring a prayer. Pierre examined Louise's face; it was inexpressive, as usual. But when he looked at her hands, he saw that she was extremely tense. The co-pilot came up to Pierre. 'Jump in ten minutes.' The plane continued to pitch around, surrounded by flak. The passengers were sporadically lit up by nearby explosions. Pierre took out a flask of whisky and gulped down a large mouthful. To his surprise, Louise grabbed it and also took a gulp, then passed it to Suzy, then to Jeanne, and finally to Gaëlle, who refused it.

'This is the time to make a vow,' Gaëlle said. 'If we survive, what would you like to do when we get back to London? Quick, answer without thinking, the first wish that comes to mind.'

Pierre rolled his eyes. 'Do you really think this is the time?'

Jeanne spoke first. 'I want to be decorated, just to imagine my mother's face if she should some day see the photo.'

Suzy suddenly became enthusiastic. 'And I'd like to dance again in front of a huge audience, with my name in big letters on the billboard!'

'What about you, Louise, what would you like to do more than anything?'

Louise answered immediately: 'Win the war.'

The explosions gradually became less frequent. The plane started a slow descent to stabilize itself. A red signal lamp lit up. The co-pilot opened the hatch.

'My God, it's now, this is it!' Suzy was feverish again. At Pierre's command, the women got up and hooked their parachutes' lines to the metal cable.

'Equipment check.'

Louise glanced at her buckle. 'Number 4 ready!' In front of her, Suzy, number 3, was virtually paralyzed. Louise elbowed her. 'Come on, let's go!'

Pierre hooked her line on and shouted, 'Number 3 ready!'

Jeanne and Gaëlle followed. Pierre noticed that Gaëlle was still wearing her gold chain around her neck. 'No personal objects!' he barked. Without protesting, Gaëlle took off the chain. 'Before you hit the ground, remember to get ready to roll.' The co-pilot came towards them with his arm lifted. The signal light changed.

'Action stations, go!'

Gaëlle jumped first, then Jeanne. Suzy closed her eyes and leapt into the void. Louise went next, as if pulled out. Pierre was the last to jump. The door closed and the bomber started to climb. Beneath it, the parachutes floated down towards the Normandy country-side. At two minutes before midnight on 30 May 1944, they landed on French soil.

Heindrich

In the early dawn, Karl already felt that this was going to be a great day. For the first time in several months, Liliane had not haunted his dreams that night. He was able to concentrate better, and God knew he needed all his perceptiveness. After making a rapid mental calculation, he realized that the date, 31 May, corresponded to his lucky number. It could be analyzed into $31+5+1944=1980$, which could then be reduced to $1+9+8+0=18$, or in sum $1+8=9$. And he had never known anything bad to happen on days numbered nine, and in fact many of those days were the happiest of his life: his entrance into the Lichterfelde officer training school, which Göring had also attended, on 3 September 1923; his arrival at the counter-espionage office; his meeting with Liliane...Thus he was not surprised when Volker announced that they might have found the British geologist.

'Last night, in the military hospital at Pont-l'Évêque, a soldier heard the man in the next bed speaking English in his delirium. He immediately informed the supervisor. The wounded man is registered under the name of Hermann Wasser, a corporal who was seriously burned during an RAF bombardment near Lisieux.'

'In other words, very near the place where the geologist's equipment was found,' Karl noted as he perused the report.

'Precisely, Colonel. I've had some checking done. The real Corporal Wasser has brown hair, and the one who is in the hospital is a redhead. I think there is a very good chance that this is our man.'

Karl and Volker looked at each other in silence. Both of them knew how much was at stake in this discovery.

'Get my car ready, we're leaving immediately.'

'Yes Sir, Colonel.'

As they drove through Normandy, the good omens were confirmed. Karl was constantly finding nines hidden in the countryside, in the number of carriages in a train or on the numberplates on the vehicles they met. Everything was going well, then: he'd never seen so many signs at once. Had his luck finally come back? Karl had always believed in the alternation of good and bad cycles. Generally speaking, every three years something happened that took him in a good or a bad direction. There was nothing he could do to prevent that. The last period had begun when he met Liliane; it was worst of all, because the bad had always been disguised as the good. Logically, that period would end this week, with the discovery of the geologist. All that made sense. Moreover, didn't cells also renew themselves in accordance with regular cycles? He just had to continue to believe.

An hour and twenty minutes later, as he was passing through the gates of the hospital, which was situated slightly outside the town, Karl noticed two nurses, and then six other people who were removing lighting equipment from an ambulance van. Three men and five women: eight! Too bad, he thought for a moment. The director of the hospital, a plump man whose forehead had beads of sweat on it, came immediately to greet him.

'Good day, Colonel. Please excuse the inconvenience. A troupe from Le Havre is going to put on a show for the patients.'

'A show? What kind of show?'

The director blushed slightly. Embarrassed, he stammered, 'It's a... that is, the men's morale being so low, I thought that... it's a number people have been talking about... I sent an ambulance to bring them here... La Femme et la Bière... Haven't you heard of it?'

The woman and beer? What in the world was this clown talking about?

Seeing the way Karl was looking at him, the director turned pale and mumbled, 'You... Perhaps you'd prefer that I cancel the performance... Would that be better for you?'

Karl reflected for a moment. The idea of a show greatly displeased him. At the same time, who would suffer from the cancellation? The poor crippled buggers who were vegetating here without any distraction. They might have been waiting for weeks for these jokers to arrive. He didn't want to penalize them or make himself unpopular. This day had begun so well, made sunny by so many nines.

'Let them have their fun. I just want the suspect to be transferred to a quiet place where I can interrogate him.'

'He's already under surveillance in a secure place, Colonel.'

Karl asked to meet the patient who had identified the suspect. In a large room filled with beds, the injured men stood at attention when they saw his uniform. Some of them had lost a leg, others an arm, an eye, sometimes more. Heindrich was touched. He had to do something.

The director led him to the bed of a corporal who had lost both legs and his vision as well during the bombardment of Lisieux. Seeing his horribly mutilated body, Karl felt tears welling up in his eyes. The man's pathetic condition hadn't prevented him from doing his duty and denouncing a traitor. He had to make a gesture. All these men were expecting that of him.

'What's your name, Corporal?' Karl asked.

'Corporal Heinz Ballhaus, Colonel.'

'Corporal Ballhaus, you will be promoted to the rank of lieutenant.'

They all applauded in unison. Karl found himself acclaimed by a group of wounded men who were about to attend a strip-tease show. It all seemed so implausible. Through the window, he saw the troupe, which was about to finish unloading the van. He also saw the two nurses talking to the taller of the two men with the van.

'Take me to the prisoner,' Karl commanded.

The suspect had been put in an upstairs room guarded by a soldier. Karl thought the place too close to the ward. If the interrogation went nowhere, as he was sure it would, he would be compelled to use force. He didn't want the whole hospital hearing the prisoner's screams. He was about to ask the director to choose a new location when he realized that the Femme et la Bière dance number could work to his advantage. 'Leave me alone with the prisoner.'

In this room with crumbling walls, a strong odour of urine attacked his nostrils. In the middle, strapped to a bed, lay the man registered under the name of Hermann Wasser. He must have been vegetating like that for some time. His forehead still bore the marks of blows. The soldiers had taken advantage of the situation to beat him up.

Karl didn't like that. He walked around the bed without saying anything. The man followed him with his eyes, on the defensive.

'What is your name?' Karl asked in English. The prisoner kept silent, as if he hadn't understood. Karl called the guard. 'Stand the prisoner's bed up against the wall, vertically.' The man couldn't repress a grimace when the guard's powerful arms lifted the bed by its frame and stood it up on two legs. Music began to filter in; the show had just started. Perfect.

After the guard left the room, Karl approached the wounded man, whose vertical position was extremely uncomfortable for him. 'Why would a British geologist come to take sand samples on a beach in Normandy? Might it have something to do with the Allied offensive? Or with this?' Karl showed the man the photos of the blocks of concrete that he had discussed at von Rundstedt's offices. The prisoner ignored the question. 'You know,' Karl went on, 'I have colleagues at the Gestapo who will make you talk anyway… I'm a soldier like you. And a soldier has to do his duty; mine is to make you talk. Sincerely, I'd like to do that without making you suffer. What were you doing on that beach?'

Since the prisoner still refused to say anything, Karl crushed out his cigarette on the man's torso. The man shrieked with pain and then struggled furiously, making the bed vibrate. 'You forced me to do that,' Karl said. 'If you don't want my next cigarette in your eye, I'd advise you to answer me.' The prisoner was now trembling with fear. Karl saw that, but he also saw a savage determination in the depth of the man's eyes. The fellow was prepared to go the distance; he had to break him quickly and completely. He grabbed an iron bar.

'What were you doing on that beach?' The suspect lowered his head, refusing to meet Karl's eyes. This time he'd asked for it, it was his own fault. Karl pulled off the Englishman's blankets. Then, as if mad, he struck the man's knees with the bar until he felt a bone break. The prisoner was howling now. Would the music from the refectory hide his screams? So what if he was heard? This might be a turning point in the war.

His body wracked by spasms, the prisoner vomited on himself. His head sank to his breast. Had he lost consciousness? Karl took his pulse and realized that his heart was beating furiously. He'd have to take a break and let the man recover. The idea of watching the prisoner wallow in his own vomit nauseated him. He needed to get some air. Then he heard the guard's voice outside the door. Somebody was trying to get in. Karl decided to see who it was. It turned out to be one of the two nurses he'd noticed as he arrived at the hospital. She was trying to force her way in, and seemed extremely indignant.

'Let me through, this patient needs care. This is inadmissible, Colonel.'

'What are you talking about?'

'This patient whom you're abusing. You're in a hospital, not a slaughterhouse. You can't behave like that.'

Karl looked at her carefully. She was about thirty years old, and the coldness of her face contrasted with the energy that seemed to be boiling within her. He was going to calm her down. 'I forbid you to enter this room, do you understand?'

Livid, her fists clenched, the nurse lowered her gaze. Karl noticed that she was making a great effort to control herself. He could have reacted more violently and made her sorry to have defied him. But he had other things to do, and didn't want to waste his energy. He moved past her without even looking at her, and started down the stairway. The show was at its climax, and the wild clamour of the spectators almost drowned out the music. Karl decided to see what was going on.

When he opened the door to the refectory, a wave of suffocating heat struck him in the face, despite the two open windows. Almost all the patients were crowded around the stage and were noisily encouraging the dancers. Some had even brought their IVs with them. On the staging two women, half-naked, were miming sexual acts. Looking more carefully, Karl realized that they were not simulating at all. The one who was kneeling with her back to him was giving the other great pleasure by caressing her breasts. The woman's shoulders reminded him of Liliane's. He immediately drove that absurd, incongruous idea out of his mind.

He hadn't thought about Liliane for a single instant. Why now? He mustn't remain even a minute longer looking at this pitiable spectacle. The two strip-tease dancers abandoned themselves to pleasuring each other, paying no attention to the raucous presence of the audience and the bawdy song coming from an old phonograph. Karl's eyes kept returning to the shoulders of the woman on her knees. He felt sweat beading on his forehead, and then he was overcome by violent nausea. He rushed out of the room, bumping into the nurse he'd kicked out of the room upstairs. There was something about her he didn't like. A nurse should never have challenged him the way she did. A nun, maybe, but not a French nurse.

He spotted the loo at the end of the hall. He didn't want to vomit in the corridor, and especially not in front of that woman. Hurrying, he managed to reach the WC before throwing up his whole breakfast. His face was sweating profusely. For some time he remained motionless, blotting his lips with his handkerchief and breathing deeply.

He was going to go back up and interrogate the prisoner. Having an empty stomach would make him harder. Before he pulled the chain, he noticed a bit of adhesive tape hanging from the ceiling. It was wrapped around the string holding up the bulb, and Karl could see a number written on it in black ink, but he could quite tell what it was. He was sure it was a 9, he could almost see it. He had to check. If it was a 9, then the wounded man would tell him what he wanted to know.

Stepping on the toilet bowl, he was able to reach the bulb. Yes, indeed, it was a 9. He didn't have time to savour his discovery before he heard a muffled sound and at the same time felt a searing pain shoot through his thigh. A second burst of shots pierced the door. Who had fired the silenced shots? Karl tried to get out, but the handle was stuck. He drew his pistol and broke the door down.

Louise

As soon as she saw her in the middle of the field where she had just landed, Louise recognized that Maria was a kindred spirit. Her lively walk, her luminous face, the fire in her eyes all reminded her of Christina Granville in London.

'Four angels who've come to make lace,' Maria cried, as a sort of welcome.

Pierre walked towards Maria to hug her. Seeing the discreet kiss they exchanged, Louise understood that they had been lovers. For once, her brother had good taste, she thought. Two other Maquisards, Bernard and René, helped them fold their parachutes and then drove them in a van to an isolated farmhouse. Sitting in front of a very thick vegetable soup served by Bernard's wife, Jeanne and Suzy could not repress a sceptical pout. Gaëlle said nothing. Every time she looked at her, Louise felt guilty. In Beaulieu, Pierre had confided to her that Gaëlle was not fooled by the trick they'd concocted to convince her to accompany them. As they went down into the cellar where they were to spend the night, Louise cornered Gaëlle. 'I think we have to talk.'

'If you want,' Gaëlle replied.

'I know that you ... about Pierre and you ... I'm the one who asked him to seduce you. If you're going to be angry at someone, it should be me, not him.'

'You don't think we have more important things to do?'

'I wouldn't want that memory to affect your commitment. You might feel resentful and put the mission in danger.'

'Pierre didn't get me to come, you know. But God did! I knew He had put you on my path. I didn't understood at first, but don't worry, I'm not angry at you.' Gaëlle turned her back on Louise and calmly started down the wooden ladder leading to her pallet.

Louise's attention was attracted by a strange metallic sound: Maria was sending a radio message. 'I've informed Buckmaster that the package was received in good condition,' she explained, amused.

'Do you know Buck well?'

'No. I don't know anyone who can claim to know him well. Even your brother...'

'You seem to know my brother well, on the other hand.'

Maria smiled broadly as she placed her radio in an old valise with a false bottom. 'We've done several missions together. He's a straight-shooter. He has told me a lot about you.'

Surprised, Louise wanted to learn more. 'He has? And what has he said?'

Maria looked at her mischievously. 'That you were the man he would have liked to be.'

Louise couldn't help smiling in turn. But she found the remark rather harsh, and was astonished that Pierre could say something like that. When Maria passed in front of her on her way to the stairs, Louise followed her. 'I'd have preferred to meet you in other circumstances. We're not going to have a long time to get acquainted.'

Still smiling, Maria looked at her. 'After the mission, we'll feel as though we've always known each other. There's nothing better than war for doing that!' She patted Louise on the shoulder and went down the stairs.

The next morning, the team went out on the road to meet the ambulance carrying the cabaret troupe. Through their contacts,

Bernard and René had learned that the troupe was expected at the hospital at four p.m. They decided to set up an ambush at the edge of Pont-l'Évêque. Eugene and two other Maquisards joined them. Gaëlle, Jeanne and Suzy hid behind trees. They didn't have to wait long. Pierre, dressed as a German soldier, stopped the van and checked the identities of the passengers sitting in front. Bernard and René slipped into the rear of the van to capture the two dancers, the dresser, and the stagehand. The driver and the passenger tried to react, but Pierre dealt with them. In less than ten minutes, they were all tied up and left with Eugene, who took them to a secret location where they were to remain until the operation was finished. Pierre had ordered that they be kept alive, but in an emergency Eugene alone would make the decision.

Maria and Louise, disguised as nurses, arrived by bicycle at the hospital just after the van. While the guard laboriously checked all the passes, Louise saw Jeanne, Gaëlle, Suzy and Pierre unloading the equipment. Bernard and René helped them. When the guard seemed suspicious, Maria exploded: 'She's replacing Lucienne, I informed the management here. Go and ask if you don't believe me.' Louise felt her hands sweating. She glanced at Suzy, who was white as a sheet. Would she be able to go on stage? Clasping her hands behind her back, Louise let her eyes wander over the hospital and the surrounding countryside, thinking that these images might the last ones she would ever see. She could be dead in a few minutes, and she accepted that. She felt frightened and serene, a duality that had been with her all her life.

A car came into the courtyard. The guard left them to go up to the big, black Citroën saloon. The driver lowered the window and said in German, 'Colonel Heindrich, Secret Services in Paris.' The guard gave the Nazi salute and lifted the barrier. Louise had time to see the face of the man sitting in the rear seat of the car. Despite the reflections on the windowpane, his cap and his turned-up collar, she recognized the Nazi officer who was posing alongside Suzy in the photos in her file. Louise's heart started to pound. It was certain that Heindrich was here because of the geologist. If he found himself face-to-face with Suzy, the whole operation could turn into a disaster.

The guard came back, gave a last glance at their papers, and let them through. Louise suddenly felt dizzy, and stumbled. 'Are you all right?' Maria said, steadying her.

Louise whispered, 'Find the package. I've got to talk to my brother.'

She went back to the van, where Pierre was finishing the unloading. 'We've got a problem. Suzy's former lover is here.'

Pierre froze. He hadn't seen Heindrich drive into the courtyard. Discreetly, he turned to look towards the steps leading to the hospital entrance, where the director was speaking to the colonel. 'Are you sure?'

'I'm sure. He's the officer in the photo. The SS must have discovered the geologist.'

'They won't leave with him.'

Louise was getting impatient. 'And if he runs into Suzy … did you think of that?'

'We're going to ensure that he doesn't see her.'

'Did Buck choose Suzy because of Heindrich? Tell me everything!'

'Go back to Maria – that's an order!'

Louise gritted her teeth; she really felt they were heading for catastrophe. Under her blouse, she felt her pistol against her belly.

She put her hand on it and went into the ward where the seriously injured patients lay. Heindrich was there, talking with a wounded man who was not the geologist. Could he have come to see someone else? The director of the hospital and several members of the staff were standing behind him. The colonel was holding the patient's hands, and had a compassionate smile on his lips. He was a rather handsome man, with a sweet face and regular features. But Heindrich belonged to the SS, and SS men were not humans. His attractive looks made him all the more terrible to Louise. She gripped the handle of her weapon. Her heart was beating wildly. On her left, in the refectory, the other patients were waiting for the show to begin. They were tapping the floor with their crutches and bellowing bawdy songs. The show would start in a few minutes. She still hadn't managed to find the geologist. Maria joined her and murmured, 'They've transferred the geologist to the upper floor. There's a guard at his door. Getting him shouldn't be too difficult.'

On their right, Heindrich was leaving the ward, followed by two soldiers. Louise and Maria stepped discreetly aside, and saw him go up the stairway.

'That officer's name is Heindrich. He mustn't see Suzy, under any circumstances,' Louise said.

'Why?'

'I don't have time to explain. Wait for me here.'

In the refectory, the music was starting up. Behind the curtain, Gaëlle had put on a record of 'Paris chéri', and in the wings Suzy and Jeanne were getting ready to make their entrance. Suzy was sweating heavily. Jeanne threw her a worried look. 'Everything all right, baby?' Suzy grabbed a bottle of cognac and took a long swig.

84

'In fifty seconds, you begin,' Gaëlle whispered to them. 'Are you ready?'

Jeanne patted her on the shoulder. 'We are, but I've got some advice for you, Bernadette Soubirous: turn your eyes away, this might be shocking for you.'

At that moment Louise burst into the dressing room. 'Suzy, I have to talk to you.' Alarmed, the dancers stared at her.

'We don't have time, we have to go on right now,' Suzy said. Louise took her by the arm, and by the way she gripped it Suzy knew that she wasn't joking.

'Keep your back to the audience as much as you can. Don't ask questions, just do as I say!'

Looking at her watch, Gaëlle gave them the signal. 'Now!'

Suzy and Jeanne hugged before going on stage. In the refectory, the patients greeted them with raucous applause. Gaëlle looked at Louise questioningly. 'What's going on, Louise?'

'Take care of the cars, the rest doesn't concern you.'

Louise crossed the refectory. Suzy and Jeanne were beginning their strip-tease. Suzy turned her back to the audience, as she had been ordered to do. The two dancers took off their clothes like two true professionals, following the steps Mrs Lynn had taught them. The patients in the front row gaped open-mouthed in delight. One of them caught Jeanne's glove when she threw it off, and this ignited a brief fight for the precious object. Jeanne removed her jacket, revealing her breasts. When she sat in a wicker chair and threw her head back, the hall fell silent. Suzy had just let her dress fall to the floor. She now wore her garter and a black bra. With her back still to the audience, she unhooked her bra and threw it over her head far into the audience, where eager hands reached out to catch it.

Louise hurried to catch up with Maria at the foot of the stairs. Terrifying shrieks of pain were coming from the upper floor. Going up the stairs, Louise asked Maria to find a stretcher. Then she went to the geologist's room and saw the guard standing at the door. 'Let me through. Someone's in pain, and he needs help!' In German, the soldier told her that no one was allowed to go in, Colonel's orders. The door opened and Heindrich was there. Calmly but firmly, Louise stood up to him. The colonel told her to go away and above all not to attempt to come in again. Louise turned on her heel and pretended to leave while he disappeared down the stairway. Taking cover in a doorway, she screwed the silencer onto her pistol, and then walked back towards the prisoner's room, the weapon hidden under her blouse. The guard moved forward to block her way. Louise shot twice, right in the heart. The man crumpled with a surprised expression on his face. Louise caught him as he fell and dragged his body into the room.

The geologist was delirious. Louise immediately understood that he didn't have long to live. She spoke to him in English. 'Don't be afraid, I've been sent by the SOE. We're going to get you out of here.' She took a syringe from her pocket and injected him with a tranquilizer. Through the window giving onto the court-yard, she saw Gaëlle under a car, placing her explosives. A German sentry was moving towards her, his rifle in his hand. Louise's heart almost stopped. If Gaëlle was captured, the whole operation would fail. She pulled the needle out of the patient and was getting ready to open the window when Pierre came up behind the sentry and cut his throat. Louise watched with great relief as he hid the body under the vehicle while Gaëlle completed her task.

At the same moment, Louise heard a sound; someone was coming. She turned around and pointed her pistol at the door. Maria appeared with the stretcher and pointed to her watch to indicate that time was short. Then she spotted the photos of the blocks of concrete and immediately removed them. Louise put a new clip into her weapon and said, 'I'll be back.'

She ran down the stairway to look for Heindrich, whom she saw in the refectory, watching the show. Now Jeanne and Suzy, still with her back to the audience, were performing sex acts on the stage. Heindrich looked upset. He put his handkerchief to his mouth and then ran staggering down the corridor to the toilet and locked himself in a stall. Noiselessly, Louise followed him, after making sure that there were no soldiers around. Heindrich was vomiting. Perfectly in control of herself, Louise went to stand in front of the toilet stall occupied by the colonel and fired four shots through the door. Then she blocked it and fired two more shots. In complete silence, she quickly left to rejoin Maria on the upper floor. She took the steps two at a time.

In the refectory, the women were finishing up their number; Suzy was emptying a pint of beer over Jeanne's body. The music stopped suddenly, and they struck a pose to signal the end. Even the most disabled patients struggled to their feet with the help of their crutches or a nurse. Others banged their spoons against their dixies, making a deafening sound. In the first row, a flashbulb went off, blinding Suzy. Jeanne saw a nurse taking pictures. Instinctively, she hid her face. Backstage, Gaëlle was ready. In her hands she held the smoke grenades that were going to cover their escape. She kept her eyes fixed on the open door to the refectory, in which Pierre's silhouette could be seen. When he saw Maria and Louise appear at the top of the stairway with the geologist on a stretcher, he gave the signal. The nurse who was taking pictures saw Jeanne and Suzy put on gas masks, and thick smoke filled the refectory. Convinced, like all the other spectators, that this was the climax of the show, he broke into laughter, and took a last picture. But soon they all realized that this was not part of the show. Patients threw themselves to the floor, coughing, amid soldiers who were blundering about with their eyes burning. Jeanne, Suzy and Gaëlle fled.

They had to act quickly. Louise and Maria were supposed to take the wounded man to the van. Despite the uproar, they could hear explosions coming from the toilets. A soldier who had not attended the show emerged at the end of the corridor. Pierre eliminated him with a burst of submachine-gun fire as he covered his comrades' escape. René loaded the geologist into the rear of the van, and Jeanne, Suzy and Gaëlle got in as well. More and more soldiers overcome by the smoke were coming into the courtyard. Panicky, they fired in all directions. René was hit in the thigh and collapsed. Bernard and Pierre shot back at the moment that the first cars exploded, knocking many of the German soldiers to the ground.

Heindrich, apparently uninjured, appeared on the hospital steps, pistol in hand. Maria shot at him several times but just missed him. Taking cover behind the body of one of his men, the colonel was barking commands, ordering a radio man to call for reinforcements. But all the radio operators had been killed. That was when Louise realized that Heindrich was still alive. She tore off her gas mask, grabbed a submachine-gun, and aimed it at him. But when she pulled the trigger, the gun jammed. Heindrich immediately spotted her and looked her straight in the eye. Five more soldiers appeared, and Heindrich opened fire on Louise. Bullets whistled past her, and she turned round to see a soldier aiming a rifle at her. At the last moment, Jeanne saved her by killing the soldier with a bullet in the forehead. There were two further explosions as Louise climbed into the van, which backed up and smashed through the barrier at the entrance to the hospital.

On the stairs, a German soldier was taking the colonel his field radio. Heindrich immediately called the Wehrmacht in Pont-l'Évêque to ask for reinforcements and to report the escapees. The nurse appeared at his side; not without a certain pride, he informed the officer that he had photographed the show.

Night was falling as the van drove through the countryside. Bernard, who had taken the wheel again, turned off on a dirt road that led into the undergrowth. A few hundred metres further and they would reach the clearing where the plane for London was supposed to pick them up. Less than ten minutes had passed since they had roared out of the hospital.

In the back of the van, Maria was putting a tourniquet on René, whose wound seemed to be superficial. After effusive hugs, the women, happy still to be alive, fell into a profound silence. They knew that only the plane could deliver them from this nightmare. Pierre tried to reassure them, but they were sweating with fear. Louise was holding the geologist's hand. He continued to moan, despite the injection. Only Gaëlle seemed serene.

'This is the time to make a promise,' she said. 'Give me your hands, quickly.' Ignoring their surprise, she took Louise's and Jeanne's hands, and then Maria's and Suzy's. 'If we don't ever see each other again, on the day the war is over, when victory has been declared, if I'm still there I'll go to a church to light a candle for each of you, even if I don't know what's happened to you. Promise me to do the same.'

This time, Suzy and Jeanne traded a look of complicity. 'We promise,' they said in unison.

'I promise, too,' Maria said. Louise remained silent.

'Well, Louise, it's your turn,' Gaëlle said.

Louise replied, 'Nothing and no one will ever make me go into a church again.' A silence followed. Louise's face expressed such intransigence that it seemed pointless to insist.

'A pencil, please ... give me a pencil.' The geologist had risen up a bit on his stretcher. Pierre gave him a pencil and a piece of paper. With a trembling hand, the man scribbled a few words. Kneeling beside him, Louise read them as he wrote: 'German officer knows about Phoenix. Kill him!' Pierre grabbed the paper and examined it with a grim look on his face.

'What does that mean?' Louise asked. Pierre didn't reply. They had just arrived at their destination. The van stopped under the trees at the edge of the clearing. Before getting out, Pierre asked Bernard to set up the beacons marking the landing area. He ordered the women to stay where they were, and signalled to Louise that she should follow him. She asked again: 'Phoenix. What does that mean? Why did he write that word?'

Pierre stopped, embarrassed. 'I can't tell you about that.'

'You can't? It's like Heindrich. If I hadn't recognized him, he might have seen Suzy and then we'd all be dead. When are you going to stop lying to me? Don't you ever trust anyone? You haven't changed.' She abruptly turned around to go back to the others, but he caught her sleeve. Behind them, the first beacons were being lit.

'The mission isn't over. There's a second part to it. We have to liquidate Heindrich. We still have a chance to catch him in Paris.'

Louise stared at him, stunned. 'In Paris? You want to send us to Paris? With Suzy, who could be recognized at any time?'

'That's why she was chosen. Heindrich won't harm her. She'll protect us.'

Louise was stupefied. 'You want to use Suzy as bait? That's the second part of the mission? She won't have the nerve.'

Now it was Pierre's turn to lower his eyes; he couldn't face his sister.

'The women fulfilled their contract,' Louise went on. 'Let them go, and we'll manage without them.'

'Maria, René and I are leaving for Paris tonight,' Pierre insisted. 'Bernard will take the rest of you to spend the night at the hideout. You will join us tomorrow. The meeting place is the Duroc Institute for the Blind; the directress is one of us.'

'But the women will be risking their lives!' Louise protested.

Without turning a hair, Pierre replied, 'Agents die on assignment every day.'

Louise couldn't restrain herself any longer, and slapped her brother. 'You'd never do this to men,' she shouted, starting back towards the van. The sound of a motor in the sky indicated the plane's arrival.

Jeanne was the first to see it start its descent towards the runway marked out by the beacons. 'Hey, girls, here's the taxi for Buckingham!'

The other women came out, followed by Bernard and René, carrying the wounded man on his stretcher. Everyone crowded around the plane that had just landed. Pierre intervened to keep the women away, with Louise behind him. 'The mission isn't over. We're expected in Paris tomorrow. Only the wounded man goes back to London.'

Jeanne thought he was joking, and laughed heartily. 'He's a bloody clown, that one. Come on, out of the way, dearie!'

'I'm not joking. You're staying here.' A leaden shroud fell over the group. Suzy began to panic. Bernard and René carried the geologist on board the plane. Jeanne attacked Louise.

'Why aren't you saying something? Did you know about this too?'

'No, I've just learned about it, like you.'

'I don't believe it. You've really fucked us over. You're no better than he is.'

'I kept my word, you have to keep yours. Nobody ever talked about going to Paris,' Suzy groaned; she seemed to be cracking like an eggshell.

For the first time in ages, Louise felt tears welling up in her eyes. Suzy rushed forward to get on the plane, but Pierre stopped her, knocking her to the ground. Gaëlle, who had not reacted, kept her eyes fixed on the plane, which was getting ready to take off. Unable to contain herself, Suzy became hysterical, and Louise and Maria had a hard time calming her down. Jeanne took Suzy in her arms, and when her eyes met Louise's she hissed between her teeth, 'What you're doing is disgusting.' She held Suzy to her for a long time. Pierre tried to remain distant.

'Hurry up and get back to the hideout,' he ordered coolly. 'We've lost enough time.'

With his rifle slung over his shoulder, Bernard started walking, immediately followed by Gaëlle. After a moment's hesitation, Suzy and Jeanne, resigned, fell in after them. Louise came last, carrying the valise filled with money. In the distance she saw Maria who was waving to them. She did not respond. Bernard had them take a path that cut across the forest. They walked single file, without saying a word. Gaëlle decided to break the silence. 'What are we going to do in Paris?'

'They'll tell us tomorrow. I don't know any more than that,' Louise lied.

'And after Paris?' Jeanne asked. 'Where else are they going to send us? To Berlin, to shoot the Führer? Really, this could go on for a long time – since we're here anyway, we might as well…'

Pierre, Maria and René were about to get back in the van when they were dazzled by a vehicle's headlights. Maria automatically fell to the ground, but Pierre and René, suddenly vulnerable, hesitated for a fatal second. 'Put down your weapons and walk towards me with your hands in the air,' Heindrich shouted. His silhouette could now be seen backlit by the headlights.

Seeing the look René gave him, Pierre understood that he was going to try something. He attempted to stop him, but René was already brandishing his submachine-gun. Although he'd been wounded, he was able to get off a burst before being cut down by an enemy volley. Pierre threw himself to the ground and put his cyanide capsule in his mouth. Two soldiers grabbed him by the shoulders and made him spit the pill out before he could swallow it.

Louise was the first to hear the gunfire. Jeanne and Suzy walked faster, followed by Gaëlle. Bernard indicated that they should stop. 'Stay here, I'll go and see.'

'No, let me go,' Louise begged. She ran back along the path, pistol in hand. She was overcome by a terrible premonition that abruptly threw her several months into the past, to the freight yard in Bourg-en-Bresse where she'd seen Claude shot down in front of her eyes. She didn't want to endure the same horror with her brother, who had never seemed so close to her. In less than a minute, she was back at the clearing. What she found there almost made her cry out. René was dead and Pierre, wounded in the leg, was being dragged towards Heindrich by two SS men. Her pulse raced. She knew that she was losing control over herself. But she couldn't resist, and she raised her arm to take aim at Heindrich. She was about to pull the trigger when Maria came up behind her and stopped her with a single look. Louise felt her heartbeat becoming more regular as she watched Pierre being pushed into the colonel's car, which immediately drove off.

The two women rejoined the others. Bernard did not take them back to the hideout where they had spent the preceding night. No one thought that Pierre would talk under torture, but Maria didn't want to take any risks. They stayed in the ruins of a bombed-out farmhouse. In the abandoned stable, Maria deciphered the message she'd just received by radio from London. Louise watched her in silence. Behind her, Suzy, Gaëlle and Jeanne were warming themselves at the fire Bernard had made.

'Has the mission been confirmed?' Louise asked.

'Yes,' Maria admitted, 'and you'll spend the night here. Bernard is going to take me to Lisieux, and then he'll come back here to get you…I'm going to Paris to make preparations for your arrival. Tomorrow morning, you'll take the first train. Tonight, you sleep in the cellar. It's safer…' Maria got up; her radio was now put away in her valise. She noticed that Louise looked lost. 'I'm sorry about your brother.'

'Pierre and you?' Louise asked. 'Was there something between you two?'

Maria nodded. Louise went up to her and took her in her arms.

'We'll see each other in Paris. Good luck!' Maria went back to Bernard, who was waiting at the door. They disappeared into the night.

'Would it kill that wop to say goodbye?' Jeanne grumbled. She was still warming herself at the fire.

Louise opened a trap door leading to the cellar, and asked the others to go down. The women resisted; they were cold, and preferred to sleep next to the hearth. Louise put out the fire to persuade them to hide in the cellar. She lit her hurricane lamp, took one last look around, and then went to join the others. At the back of the cellar, Suzy, Gaëlle and Louise lay in silent hostility, immobile in the dark among empty bottles and apple crates. Jeanne was walking up and down to warm herself, her eyes fixed on the valise full of cash that Louise kept close by her.

'Could you stop pacing like that? You're making me dizzy,' Suzy complained.

'To think that we're freezing our arses off on a pile of rotten apples when we've got millions of francs in small bills… This might be the time to use some of that cash, don't you think?'

Gaëlle chimed in: 'How can you think about money at a time like this?'

'What do you expect? It's my nature, I was born a whore just as you were born with a silver spoon in your mouth, my angel…'

To everyone's surprise, Gaëlle seized Jeanne by the collar and threw her against a bottle rack. 'You mean that you're used to being humiliated, right? Do you realize what you're doing to yourself by despising yourself? Do you realize?'

Jeanne didn't react immediately; she was stunned by Gaëlle's sudden explosion. 'I must be dreaming! The way she talks! Go back to your rosary!' Jeanne pushed Gaëlle away. Louise came between them to prevent Gaëlle from being punched.

'Buck is ordering us to go to Paris. All four of us will go, without arguing, is that understood?'

'I don't care a damn about Buckmaster,' Suzy said. 'I'm not in the Resistance and I'm not a spy. You should've hired professionals; you've betrayed us, I can't trust you any more.'

Gaëlle counter-attacked again. 'Pierre has been arrested, René is dead … It's our duty to take over for them!'

'Our duty my arse!' Jeanne shouted. 'Once the war is over, we'll be tarts or skivvies again, and no one will remember us! So I want my share now.'

Suzy came and stood behind Jeanne to support her. Jeanne took a step forward. Louise drew her pistol and pointed it at her. 'The first person who touches that money won't keep it long.'

Jeanne smirked. 'You won't shoot me … You're not like your brother!'

'You want to bet?' A heavy silence filled the cellar. They heard footsteps upstairs. Bernard, back from the station, had relit the fire. Jeanne, still smirking, took another step forward. Gaëlle and Suzy stiffened. Louise's face remained expressionless, but her hand was not trembling. Gaëlle knew that she would fire.

'Give me the valise,' Jeanne said. The sound of a motorcycle exploded in the night, immediately followed by shouts in German. The women froze. Above them, there was rifle fire. Objects fell and then submachine-guns crackled on all sides. They heard what sounded like a terrible struggle, with bodies rolling on the ground and heart-rending howls. Then it was finally silent.

Suzy was trembling. Seeing that she was going to scream, Jeanne took Suzy in her arms and put her hand over her mouth. Louise signalled that they should not move. Her pistol in her hand, she moved noiselessly towards the wooden stairway and climbed the first steps on tiptoe. She put her hand on the handle of the trap door and cracked it open. Her eyes at floor level, she could make out objects that had fallen. Through the half-open front door she saw the pale light of dawn. She opened the trap door a little further and climbed out, her pistol at the ready.

That was when she saw Bernard and the German lying in a pool of blood near a Wehrmacht motorcycle and sidecar. In his hand, Bernard still held the knife he'd used to cut his adversary's throat. The area around seemed calm, but reinforcements were certain to arrive. They had to get out of there as fast as they could. She was turning around to look for the other women when she heard a sound. In a flash, a man who'd been hidden behind the motorcycle was on her. Crushed by his weight, Louise collapsed and dropped her weapon, which flew several metres away. The soldier had drawn a knife, and Louise barely had time to grab his arm and hold it back. But he was very strong, and the knife came closer and closer to her eyes. Louise feared she wouldn't be able to hold out much longer. Within a few seconds, the knife would plunge into her eye socket, and if she were lucky she'd be killed instantly. The man seemed to be enjoying that scene in advance. Louise felt her strength giving out. She gave an angry shout and tried one last time to push her attacker away, with the force of despair. Two shots rang out behind her. Louise felt blood spurt on her mouth and nose.

The man's head had just exploded like a watermelon. The full weight of his body fell on her chest, almost suffocating her. As she rolled to the side so that she could breathe, she caught sight of Gaëlle standing in the doorway, a smoking pistol in her hand. Seeing the half-horrified, half-astonished look on her face, Louise guessed that Gaëlle had just killed her first man.

Behind them, Jeanne and Suzy, still in shock, were looking at her with gaping mouths. Louise pushed the body away and got to her feet. 'We've got to hurry,' she finally said. 'It'll soon be light.'

An hour and half later, after an exhausting trek across the fields, the women reached Lisieux, where they separated, Louise and Suzy going one way, Jeanne and Gaëlle another. At nine-thirty, they boarded the train for Paris, sitting in two different carriages. Sitting across from Suzy in a crowded compartment, Louise closed her eyes. She'd been on French soil for forty-eight hours and had had some adventures. Soon, if everything went well, the train would arrive at Saint Lazare station in Paris. On that day, 2 June, what she had denied herself up to that point suddenly happened. She fell asleep.

Pierre

Under heavy escort, the prison van carrying Pierre stopped at number 84 avenue Foch in Paris. He'd heard about what went on in that building; British SOE agents, as well as leaders of the French Resistance like Jean Moulin and Pierre Brossolette, had been interrogated and tortured there. Brossolette had taken advantage of a moment of inattention on the part of the guards to throw himself out of a lavatory window on the top floor. Pierre looked at the pavement where the poor wretch had fallen; would he have as much courage as the great Maquisard?

When they arrived at the offices of the SD – the Sicherheitsdienst, the Gestapo's counter-espionage service – the prisoner was taken up to the interrogation room. His leg was hurting him terribly. The Germans had crudely removed the bullet that had lodged in it without sewing up the wound. On the landing of the top storey, Pierre recognized Josef Goetz, who was leaning on the railing, smoking a cigarette. Buckmaster had talked to Pierre on several occasions about this man. When a British agent was captured, Goetz seized his crystal radio and sent false messages in code to the SOE in order to gather information.

Sturmbahnführer Hans-Josef Kieffer was officiating on the fifth floor. This SS officer had been informed of Pierre's capture, but Pierre discovered that he would not have to confront him, because he continued his painful climb to the sixth floor, where the staff room, the interpreter's office and a few cells were located. Karl Heindrich was waiting for him. His tired face betrayed a lack of sleep, and his stiff leg recalled the wound he'd received the day before. Behind him, a secretary wearing a suit and forage cap was sitting quietly behind a typewriter. The colonel ordered a soldier to remove Pierre's clothes. His arms were tied behind his back, and he was hung from the ceiling by a rope. The soldiers immediately tore off the clot of coagulated blood on his thigh and inserted into the wound a thin metal needle, one of four set out on the table. 'Don't worry, they've been sterilized,' Heindrich said.

Pierre, in a state of shock, let out a howl of pain that was quickly extinguished by the pail of icy water thrown in his face. A man struck him a series of blows to the face that dislocated his jaw. The taste of blood was in his mouth. The soldier who was hitting him knew what he was doing, because he stopped just before Pierre lost consciousness.

Detached and impassive, Heindrich lit a cigarette and unfolded a piece of paper that Pierre recognized at once, despite his blurred vision. 'German officer knows about Phoenix. Kill him,' Karl read. 'What does that mean?'

Pierre defied Heindrich, trying to ignore the pain tormenting him.

'I found it in your pocket,' the colonel continued. 'It was the geologist who wrote it, wasn't it?'

'I don't know what you're talking about.'

Heindrich smiled. He took a puff on his cigarette, stifled a cough, and broke out laughing, as if Pierre had just made a good joke. 'I don't know who you are, Mr SOE. But to have that kind of nerve, you're certainly not just anyone. And because you aren't, you know what's hidden behind the word 'Phoenix'. You don't want to tell me now, but you'll end up telling me everything, believe me!'

Pierre remained silent. Heindrich looked at the scars that he already had all over his torso. Then he laid the paper on the table and came up to Pierre. Pierre tensed, expecting to receive another blow. But Heindrich simply held up a photo of blocks of concrete. 'One of your accomplices stole photographs of these blocks from me. You know what they are, don't you?' Pierre didn't budge. He was having trouble breathing. 'Do they have something to do with the invasion? Answer…'

'I told you, I don't know what you're talking about.'

One of the soldiers stepped forward to strike Pierre in the stomach, but Heindrich stopped him. He spoke to Pierre in a calm, almost friendly voice, a voice that didn't betray his fatigue. 'You see these needles on the table? The first one will be slipped under your fingernails. Believe me, for someone of your kind, it's very unpleasant. If you're stubborn, the second needle will be inserted into your urethra, and you won't like that either. Finally, if you still haven't told me what I want to know, the third needle will perforate your right eye. Then you'll spend the night in your cell. Tomorrow morning, I'll come to see you with four new needles. I hate to have to resort to this sort of thing, but if you persist, you don't leave me any choice – is that clear?'

Pierre bent his head. He was overcome by fear. It would get the better of him if he continued to hold Heindrich's gaze. At that point someone knocked at the door. Without taking his eyes off Pierre, Heindrich ordered that the door be opened. Volker appeared and handed him a briefcase. 'Excuse me, Colonel, but I've received the photos you were waiting for.'

Heindrich rapidly skimmed the pictures of the show at the hospital. Most of them were blurry, and did not allow him to see the faces of the dancers clearly. 'What do you expect me to do with those? They're unusable, you can't see anything!'

'There's one that should interest you – the last one, you'll see.'

Pierre raised his head, praying that it would not be a picture of Suzy. Heindrich stopped at the last picture. Vague and poorly framed, it nonetheless made an identification possible. He held it up in front of Pierre. 'You don't know her, I suppose?' Pierre saw Gaëlle's face, peeking out from behind the curtain. He shook his head. Heindrich calmly ordered Volker to have the picture enlarged and sent to every railway station in France.

'Don't you think these women are already back in England now?'

'Now I mustn't overlook anything,' Heindrich replied. Then without further reflection he walked past Pierre and left the room, telling the others, 'Go to it. If he wants to talk, let me know.' The rope was cut and Pierre collapsed on the floor, feeling as if all his bones had just been broken. The two soldiers sniggered and mumbled incomprehensible words. One of them selected a needle while the other untied Pierre's hands. They picked him up and carried him to a chair with wooden arms, to which his wrists were firmly attached. The secretary was filing her fingernails, paying no attention to what was going on. Trying not to think about the ordeal he was about to face, Pierre forced himself to think about some happy event in his past. Curiously, it was to Le Bérail that his mind took him. He saw the paved courtyard and the great stone staircase, a perfect replica of the one at the great house in Fontainebleau. At the foot of the stairs, there was a little girl, whom he had thought forever lost in his memory. Laughing wildly, she was playing with a big dog that was licking her cheeks. Now she was calling for Pierre's help, because he was there, too, and laughing as hard as she was. He saw himself grab the dog by the collar and free the little girl. He'd never been happier than on that day more than thirty years before, when Louise had called out for his help ...

Louise

Her forehead pressed against the window of the railway compartment, Louise felt a pain growing in her belly. It wasn't fear that was producing the cramp this time, and it wasn't hunger either. She knew herself too well not to recognize that this sensation was different, something new. Sitting across from her, Suzy was watching her. Louise was definitely no longer in complete control of herself, and the idea terrified her.

'Are you all right? You don't look good...'

Louise saw Suzy's lips moving, but she couldn't catch the words as they dissolved into the air like ink into a glass of water. The nausea that gripped her was so violent that for a moment she thought she was going to vomit in front of all the other passengers. That idea made her furious. She couldn't humiliate herself that way. She had to do something.

'I'm going to get some air.'

'I'll come with you,' Suzy said, happy for a chance to escape the persistent stares of the other passengers.

At that moment they heard a whistle, followed by an abrupt application of the brakes that threw Louise and Suzy forward. Baggage fell from the overhead storage onto the passengers. A valise opened and a whole ham, carefully wrapped in a towel, flew out. A small woman sitting at the end of the banquette rushed to put it back, like a schoolgirl caught doing something she shouldn't. In the corridor, people were shouting. Louise looked to see where Buck's valise was. It had landed on the knees of the old man chewing tobacco who'd been sitting on her left. He was groaning as he tried to pick it up.

'What have you got in there?' he mumbled. Suzy turned towards him, but Louise got there first, tearing the valise out of the old man's hands.

'Don't touch that!' she said. Surprised by her own reaction, she realized that the pain had disappeared. Suzy seemed dumbfounded, and looked at her with her mouth open. 'Let's go and see what's happening,' Louise continued. The softness of her voice astonished her. Inside, she'd felt only the urge to scream. In the corridor, the heat was becoming suffocating. Travellers pressed against the windows, jostling each other. A terrified woman headed straight for Louise, shouting, 'I've lost my son! Have you seen my child?' Louise pushed her out of the way and moved on, followed by Suzy, whom all the men gaped at with desire. One woman, jealous of the attention Suzy aroused, blocked their way.

'Tart! Just look at how you're dressed – aren't you ashamed?'

'You can't do that – what's wrong with you?' Suzy replied.

'Go back to your brothel, you whore!'

The woman spat in Suzy's face. Breathless, close to tears, Suzy got hold of herself and moved on. Louise offered her a handkerchief and said simply, 'We've got to find Jeanne and Gaëlle.' Suzy nodded, wiping her cheek with the handkerchief. Around them, people were saying that the train had stopped because of an explosion on the tracks. Others had got out their carriages and were questioning the conductors, who urged them to re-board the train. Along the tracks, a woman wearing a blue dress had taken off her shoes. Beside her, a man was wiping his forehead. Behind them a young mother was helping her little girl pee. Louise looked at them and went on her way.

It was then that she saw him. On the other side of the tracks, near the clump of trees down below. Claude. He was looking at her with that rare smile that she saw only when he was proud of her. Louise froze. Curiously, the apparition of her husband surprised her less than the jacket he'd put on. It was the black corduroy one she'd bought him in Grenoble! If in a moment of mad hope, she'd believed or tried to believe that her husband was alive, she knew that that jacket couldn't be brand new. Louise had torn it off him when he was wounded the preceding January, leaving it in shreds and covered with blood among the nettles on the Hotonnes plateau. The jacket brought her back to reality. She couldn't help smiling.

'Why are you stopping?' Louise turned to look at Suzy, then looked again at the clump of trees. Claude had disappeared.

The restaurant car was in the middle of the train, and there were a dozen German officers in it. Laughing uproariously, they were listening to a hilarious story as they sat round a table covered with empty wine bottles. As soon as Suzy appeared, the talk and laughter ceased. Seeing that she had hesitated on seeing the uniforms, Louise, a few metres behind her, told her to keep going. Heaving a deep sigh, Suzy moved through the carriage without pausing. Louise followed her, gripping the handle of Buck's valise and trying not to think about what was in it.

The Germans' flushed faces expressed stupefaction and amusement. One of them raised his glass and said something that sounded like an invitation to join them. Once again, Louise felt pain in her stomach. Nausea overcame her. As she saw Suzy leaving the restaurant car, she knew she'd never make it to the door. She fainted just as she was passing the last table. A major got up to catch her as she fell. Buck's valise landed at the feet of another officer, who immediately called for help.

Jeanne was furious. Since they'd left Lisieux, Gaëlle had been telling her about the Jesuits' and the Jansenists' differing conceptions of divine grace. She'd even tried to persuade her of the merits of the Jesuit teaching that the only sinners are those whose minds are conscious of sin. This was the last straw.

'I don't care a damn about divine grace, I'm knee-deep in shit. I like sin, I can't get enough of it. In fact, I don't even believe in God – you know why? Because my first customer was a Jesuit. I've never seen a guy as small-minded, and he was even smaller down below. So spare me your pious talk. If you want to convert somebody, you've chosen the wrong person.'

'Why didn't you tell me that I was annoying you? I would have talked about something else,' Gaëlle replied calmly.

'I don't want you to talk to me! I want you to shut up once and for all. If you say another word I'll explode in your face – and you chemists know what that means, don't you?'

'Go ahead, shout it on the rooftops, while you're at it.'

Jeanne went out into the crowded corridor. On the way, a man with a moustache caressed her buttocks. She turned around. 'Sure, don't restrain yourself – what do you take me for?'

'Not a lady, anyway.' He put his hand on her buttock again, to the great amusement of the people around him, who laughed and applauded. Jeanne gave him a violent slap. The man took a step back, lifting his hand to his cheek. Around him, the applause grew louder, this time directed at Jeanne. Surprised by so much respect, she was ready to go another round. Gaëlle didn't give her time, and pulled her to the end of the carriage.

'Do you really want to create a scene, do you think we need that?'

'The best defence is attack. I was brought up that way. That's why I'm here,' Jeanne retorted, at the same time making a hand gesture at the man. A moment later, suddenly melancholic, she added, 'And it's sad to say, but the Germans – you have to give 'em that much – they're a little better behaved than all these bastards.'

Gaëlle stared at her, speechless. At that moment, Suzy emerged from the corridor, her face pale.

'There you are,' Jeanne said. 'Do you know why we've stopped?'

'No, but that way it's full of Germans,' Suzy replied, pointing to the restaurant car, 'and they don't really look worried.'

'Where's Louise?' Gaëlle asked.

'She was behind me just a minute ago.'

The three women looked at each other in silence. They were all thinking the same thing.

'If they'd arrested her, I'd have heard her cry out. She must have been delayed,' Suzy continued.

'They might also have asked to see her papers. We've got to go and see,' Gaëlle said.

Jeanne intervened. 'Stay there, I'll go. It's better that we don't all go together.' Jeanne took Suzy with her, Gaëlle watching them suspiciously.

'She might be sick, she didn't look well,' Suzy said.

'Because you're just fine and raring to go? I've slept three hours in three days, I look like hell and I smell like an old mop. Except for that, I'm fine. Louise is no different.'

'You know she is. And I'm telling you that she's got a problem.'

The restaurant car was now half empty. A waiter was clearing the tables when Jeanne and Suzy came in. Suzy immediately noticed Buck's valise, which was sitting on a chair. She was heading straight towards it when an SS major blocked her way.

'Are you looking for something?' The man had emerged from a doorway. He was smoking a eucalyptus cigarette. His body odour mixed with a strong smell of cologne nauseated her. 'Mademoiselle?' The SS man had now recovered the valise. Suzy couldn't budge, immobilized by his steel-blue eyes. Jeanne saved her. She went up to the officer, using all her charm.

'That valise belongs to a friend of ours. We were just now looking for her; perhaps you've seen her?'

The man looked at her as he put the cigarette to his lips. 'Could you describe this friend?' The man's eyes pierced her. Jeanne retained her composure. She looked at the major's right ear, a technique she'd tried out with her first customers. It always allowed her to reverse the power relationship.

'Thirty-five, brunette, hazel eyes, wearing a brown beret.'

To her great surprise, the officer handed her the valise. 'You'll find her in the next carriage, at the end of the corridor…She fainted, and a doctor is examining her…'

'A doctor?' Suzy asked.

'Yes, Major Willteigen. He is very competent, I assure you.'

Louise was slowly regaining consciousness. A man in a German uniform was leaning over her, examining her with a stethoscope. She was lying on the banquette, in her slip. Her clothes were carefully folded over one of the arms.

'You fainted. I took the liberty of examining you. I'm a physician. How long has it been since you've eaten?'

'I...I'm afraid I don't do well in crowds...I felt ill in the corridor...It was so hot...But I'm better now,' she finally whispered.

The man smiled slightly and got up and opened a large leather bag. Louise looked around for her valise. It had disappeared. She felt fear growing in the pit of her stomach. Then the doctor handed her a bar of German chocolate. 'Here, eat a little. You've got to regain your strength.'

She tried to look calm, and sat up on the banquette. She peeled away the silvery paper and bit into the bar. The taste of chocolate filled her mouth. First-rate chocolate, such as she hadn't tasted for more than five years. The doctor didn't take his eyes off her. Louise appreciated his elegant way of treating her, keeping his distance.

'You aren't wearing a wedding ring,' he said. 'You aren't married?'

The question struck her like a blow. 'Pardon me?'

'Your husband isn't accompanying you?'

For a moment she saw Claude's phantom near the tracks, just before she'd fainted. Her eyes became veiled. 'No...he...he's not with me...not just now,' she stammered.

'He knows, I assume?'

Louise felt her concern mounting. What game was this fellow playing? Were his questions innocent, or did they mask suspicions? No doubt he'd opened the valise and found the money. Had Jeanne, Gaëlle and Suzy already been arrested? Other officers might be waiting in the corridor. She could kill the doctor, right now, using the hold she'd been taught at Beaulieu. But she'd have to take him by surprise, and he was on his guard. And then she wasn't strong enough to break his neck. Was he armed? She could draw him to her and then take his pistol.

'I was already in France when my wife got pregnant, two years ago,' the doctor continued. 'Since then I've seen my daughter only once … This war … a terrible thing, really. I hope your husband will be there when you give birth.' He put his stethoscope back in his bag. Louise suddenly felt as if a huge weight had just crushed her chest. Hypnotized by the officer's sweetness, she could say nothing for a moment.

'You … what do you mean, exactly?' He looked at her for a moment, still charming, and then his expression changed and he seemed overcome by embarrassment.

'Good Lord, you didn't know? You're pregnant, Madame, at least three months along. I'm sure, there is no doubt.' Louise wanted to reply, but she couldn't utter a sound.

Gaëlle looked at her watch. Jeanne and Suzy had left more than a quarter of an hour before. No one knew when the train would start up again. She was dying to go and look for them, and tried to find a way to calm down. Her eyes fell on the travellers gathered along the tracks. A bearded man in shirtsleeves was scratching his nose. She decided to count all the men with beards she saw. A good way to distract herself. But when the second bearded man crossed her field of vision, she changed the rules. If I find a third bearded man, then I'm going to find Jeanne and Suzy. She noted a bald man, three nuns, and a German officer who was smoking a cigarette and talking to a pretty woman, who seemed embarrassed to have to converse with him. Then Gaëlle heard a man's voice behind her. 'Pardon, Mademoiselle.'

Moving aside to let a father and his young son pass, she saw, through a crack in the door of the compartment, an old man wearing a beard like a collar. 'A collar is the same as a beard,' she said to herself, starting down the corridor towards the restaurant car.

※ ※

She found Suzy alone in the restaurant car. 'What are you doing? Have you found Louise?'

Suzy looked at her with her frightened doe's eyes. 'Apparently she fainted. A doctor is examining her... a German.'

'Shit! Where's Jeanne?'

Suzy turned around. 'She was there, not two minutes ago... with the valise.'

'The valise?'

※ ※

Jeanne climbed over the two teenagers in berets who were sitting on the carriage's steps, and found herself on the tracks, too absorbed in her thoughts to hear them whistle at her as she passed. The sight of a German soldier talking to a conductor stopped her. Holding the valise, she turned round and started walking in the opposite direction, taking care not to hurry too much. On her right, there were trees, and beyond them the road to Évreux. With a little luck, she wouldn't have to walk more than ten or twenty minutes along the road, just long enough for a car to stop. She'd really played this one well. In an hour at most, this whole business would be just a bad memory.

'Jeanne, stop. You can't do that.' Gaëlle had just caught up with her, and quickly took her under control.

'Louise is with a Boche – it's over, old girl. You do what you want; I've made my choice.'

'I thought you wanted to prove to your mother that you were worth something.'

'Oh, don't start in on your catechism again! Change the record!'

'Give me that valise.' Gaëlle slipped her hand into the pocket of her coat. Jeanne looked at it. Something was pointing through the fabric.

'What've you got in there? Your missal?'

Gaëlle shrugged. 'Maybe … not.'

The image of the German whose head had exploded came back to Jeanne for an instant. She saw Gaëlle again standing there with a smoking pistol in her hand and German's body at her feet, on top of Louise, who was covered with his blood. 'Thou shalt not kill, how about that? Twice in two days, wouldn't that be a pretty heavy burden for a pious Christian?'

'God's grace will help me – that's my preferred way, as you know.'

The train's whistle suddenly blew. 'All aboard!' shouted the conductor.

Motionless and alone, Jeanne and Gaëlle stood face-to-face. The train started up. Gaëlle didn't budge. What if all her preaching was just a bluff, Jeanne asked herself. Maybe the valise was what she really wanted. In a few seconds, the train would be far away, and no one would see Gaëlle shoot her and take off with the money. That idea was unbearable for Jeanne, and she jumped onto the carriage's steps as they passed by her. Surprised by her sudden turnaround, Gaëlle moved too late, letting the train gain speed and finding the steps out of reach. Pleased with her trick, Jeanne watched Gaëlle run, but almost immediately, moved by a reflex she couldn't have explained, she put down the valise and held out her hand. Gaëlle summoned her last strength to grasp it.

'I've got you, I won't let you go,' Jeanne told her, and pulled Gaëlle up onto the steps. Hugging her, Jeanne plunged her hand into Gaëlle's coat pocket. She found nothing in it but a handkerchief. Gaëlle smiled at her, picked up the valise, and disappeared into the compartment. Jeanne stood there speechless, and then swore.

Louise came out of the compartment with the German physician. She was pale.

'Come with me as far as the restaurant car. They're sure to have something left to eat. It will do you good. I'll pay.'

'It's all right. Thank you very much.'

'As you wish. My respects, Madame, and good luck.'

Louise waited until he'd left before heading for the WC. Just as she was about to go in, she saw Suzy in the corridor.

'Louise!' Without even stopping, she closed the door in Suzy's face and burst into tears. Suzy was pounding on the other side of the door. 'Louise, speak to me! Are you all right? What did he say to you?'

'It's nothing... I'm just tired... It'll be all right.'

'But you're crying? Are you crying, Louise?'

Louise slid down to the floor, her fist in her mouth. For the first time since the beginning of their venture, she was overcome by doubts.

The train arrived at Saint Lazare two and a half hours late. Louise had recovered, and her face no longer showed any sign of emotion. Jeanne, Gaëlle and Suzy glanced at each other furtively, but Louise remained silent. She and Suzy were the first to leave the train. Jeanne and Gaëlle followed them at a distance of a few metres. They were all to make their way separately to the Duroc Institute for the Blind. Louise spotted four German military policemen who were checking the travellers at the head of the train. One of them was holding a sheet of paper. By the movement of his eyes, which were passing from the paper to the faces of the passengers, Louise understood that he was looking at a search bulletin. Had one of them been identified? Had Pierre talked? Her heart nearly stopped, but her mind commanded her not to show anything. She slowed down, so that Jeanne and Gaëlle would catch up.

'They're doing a check up ahead. Stay calm, they may not be looking for us. We'll meet in an hour at the Institute for the Blind on the boulevard des Invalides. Be sure that you're not followed. If you can't get there, come tomorrow at noon to the Concorde metro station, direction Pont-de-Neuilly ... From now on, we don't know each other.'

They dispersed in the crowd of passengers. But seeing Suzy starting to go to pieces, Louise grabbed her hand to keep her under control. With her other hand, Louise still held fast to the SOE's valise. 'I'm sure they're looking for us. Your brother must have given us up,' Suzy moaned.

'Shut up and stay with me.' Louise smelled a familiar scent behind her. Someone took the valise out of her hand. She turned around and found herself face-to-face with the doctor who had examined her.

'Allow me, Madame,' he said, bowing.

'Thank you, doctor, that's very kind of you,' Louise was surprised to find herself replying, pulling Suzy towards her. 'I'd like to introduce you to my friend Liliane.'

'Delighted, Mademoiselle. Come with me, it's not good to queue up in your condition.' Carrying the valise, he bypassed the line of travellers, saluted the policemen, and crossed the barrier unhindered, followed by his escort. No one paid attention to the women.

A few metres further back, Jeanne was still walking along. In the crowd, she recognized the lout whom she'd slapped in the train. He had no hard feelings, and was now blowing her kisses. As she came up to the checkpoint, she undid the top button of her blouse and spotted a policeman with a stripe on his shoulder.

'Officer,' she complained, 'since Lisieux I've been bothered by that man with a moustache over there. His hands all over me, and a strange fellow, he's got something on his conscience, if you know what I mean.' Her interlocutor glanced at the fellow, who was continuing to blow kisses to all the women who passed by him.

'Don't worry, Madame, we'll check him out. Here, go ahead.'

'It's a good thing you're there,' Jeanne replied. 'I feel safe with you.' She moved through the barrier easily just as the man with the moustache, confronted by the policeman, began to draw attention to himself. Jeanne shot Gaëlle a last glance and then headed for the exit.

Alone in the line, Gaëlle felt her pulse beating faster. When she arrived in front of the man checking identities, she handed him her papers, which he inspected quickly before waving her on.

Reassured, she took back her identity card and gave him her best smile. She did not notice the nod he directed at an agent in civilian clothes. As she was going towards the entrance to the metro, she jumped as she felt the sudden pressure of a hand on her shoulder.

Heindrich

Heindrich had made it a point of honour to produce the most accurate photofit possible. However, no colour could represent the savage brilliance of the nurse's pupils, or her icy gaze full of arrogance. In his office at the Regina, he had worked for hours on a number of models. Confronted by the unsatisfactory results, he'd felt discouraged for the first time in the last forty-eight hours. The fatigue of the past few days didn't help. He was increasingly unsure that he would be able to give arguments that would convince Rommel. And the prisoner still refused to talk. Several needles had already been inserted under his nails, and one had almost perforated his urethra. Today, he'd probably lose a finger or two...all in vain. Heindrich was certain that the man would die before he admitted anything. 'Phoenix' had to have something to do with the blocks of concrete photographed by their plane, but like a man faced with the scattered pieces of a puzzle, Heindrich lacked the overall picture that would allow him to attain his goal.

'Colonel,' Volker interrupted, setting in front of him a pile of documents, 'I got these files from the Gestapo. Some of the photos might correspond to the photofit. Do you want to have a look at them?' What would he do without Volker? The fellow was really his guardian angel. Or simply very concerned about him.

Most of the photos showed Maquisards or women associated with the Resistance. None of them were of SOE agents. Without much hope, he laid them out in front of him. All at once, one profile jumped out at him. It came from a search bulletin, and concerned a certain Louise Granville, née Desfontaines, the wife of a Maquis leader in the Corlier network who'd been killed at the station in Bourg-en-Bresse at the beginning of April.

'That's the one!' Karl exclaimed. His energy returned. Like a chess player who has just discovered a winning combination, he understood that he would succeed in checkmating his opponent.

'Are you sure?' Volker said. 'That woman has not been spotted anywhere for at least two months. The Gestapo thought she was dead or had escaped to Spain.'

'She was just in England, and I'm sure she has come back. Drive me to avenue Foch. I want to interrogate the prisoner.'

Crossing the hall of the hotel, Karl was again confronted by Eddy. 'Colonel, I have to talk to you. This time I think I've got the right one.' Karl felt a mute rage come over him. How could Eddy have the nerve to approach him in the presence of his aide-de-camp?

'Volker, could you wait for me in the car? I'll just be a moment.'

'Yes Sir, Colonel.'

Karl waited until Volker had disappeared, and then grabbed Eddy by the arm and took him into the bar, which was empty at this early hour in the morning.

'Where do you think you are? Do you think you can just come in here whenever you want to talk to me about your little schemes? Do you think I don't have anything more important to do?'

Instead of replying, Eddy simply showed Karl the photo. 'You've got to admit, this time I've done it, haven't I? Tell me frankly, she's just about right, isn't she?'

Once again, the girl had nothing in common with Liliane. Looking at her vulgar pout and her whore's pose, Karl knew that he no longer wanted to have anything to do with Eddy. He tore up the photo.

'From the beginning, you have understood nothing. Now get out, I don't ever want to see you here again.'

'You can't find the double of your girlfriend just anywhere,' Eddy pleaded. 'You don't realize what you're asking of me.'

Karl looked him up and down one last time. 'I've never asked anything of you. Don't try to find excuses,' he said, heading for the revolving door.

Eddy felt miserable. The colonel had in fact never asked anything of him. More than a year before, learning that Heindrich's fiancée had disappeared on their wedding day, he'd had the idea of approaching him. Thanks to his network of informers, he was sure he could find her, and in that way be able to set up a purchasing service, the sine qua non for getting rich on the black market. Eddy had quickly become discouraged, because the woman seemed to have completely disappeared, probably eliminated by the Resistance or even by the Nazis themselves, since Heindrich had enemies within his own ranks. But then one day a chambermaid at the Regina with whom he was having an affair reported rumours regarding the officer. Heindrich had preserved intact room 813, where he and Liliane had made love. He went there almost every night to touch religiously the dresses the young woman had worn. Finally, one evening a housekeeper had surprised the colonel in the company of a prostitute, whom he was asking to put on clothes worn by his beloved. That was how Eddy came to make Heindrich a new offer: since he couldn't find Liliane, he might be able to recreate the memories by providing doubles. Eddy realized how cheeky his suggestion was, but to his great surprise the colonel agreed to it. Now, after several months of searching in vain and having presented a dozen girls, all this work was over? He couldn't accept it. As he left the Regina, his mind still stunned by the blow it had just received, Eddy didn't see the woman who was charging towards him. He hit her straight on, knocking her down and stumbling into the gutter.

'Couldn't you look where you're going?' he shouted, and then got hold of himself, enchanted by the young woman's beauty.

'Excuse me, it was my fault,' she said. 'I was thinking of something else, and didn't see you coming.' Eddy helped her to her feet. She was slender and had deep, dark eyes.

'Not at all! I reacted like a boor; allow me to make it up to you. Let me buy you a drink. You can call me Eddy. What's your name?'

'Maria,' the woman answered, taking his arm. They started walking towards the nearest café.

Pierre's head had been held beneath the water for more than a minute. Heindrich told his men to stop. They seized Pierre by the hair and threw him to the floor.

'For the last time, where is Louise Desfontaines?' Heindrich asked, crushing out his fifth cigarette.

Pierre was disfigured, but Heindrich had ordered them not to injure his eyes. He wanted the prisoner to identify Louise's photo. But it was no good. Pierre still wouldn't talk.

'Well?'

Pierre turned his aching face to Heindrich. 'I don't know her... I've never seen her.'

The colonel knelt down next to him. 'I don't want to kill you. You're a courageous man, and I respect that. But I know that you're lying, and I also know that you can't endure more suffering. Pierre remained impassive. Then he signalled to Heindrich to come closer.

The officer bent down, his heart pounding. Pierre's lips moved but did not utter a word.

'What is it? Tell me, I'm listening...'

In a final effort, Pierre spat in his face, and laughed at him. The torturers leapt on him and beat him. Heindrich stood up. He knew that the prisoner would never talk. He was torn by a sense of waste, but he told his men to finish Pierre off.

The telephone on the secretary's desk rang; Heindrich had forgotten she was even there. 'Hello? Very good, I'll put him on. Colonel, it's for you,' she cooed as she handed him the receiver.

It was Volker, telling him that one of the members of the commando, a woman, had just been arrested. Heindrich took a deep breath. So providence had not abandoned him after all. He ordered the men not to kill Pierre just yet.

Less than an hour later, Gaëlle entered the room. Seeing Pierre mutilated, she cried out.

'Mademoiselle was arrested as she got off the train from Lisieux an hour ago. I won't introduce you,' Heindrich said. One of the torturers forced Pierre to look at Gaëlle. 'If you don't care about your own pain, maybe you'll be more sensitive to that of your young friend here.'

Pierre's breathing was more regular now. His eyes fixed on Gaëlle, he looked at her without seeing her. Heindrich ordered that Gaëlle be undressed. Paralyzed, Gaëlle remained motionless while a man took off her clothes. Clad only in her stockings, she was now shivering all over. Heindrich nodded, and Gaëlle was strapped to a chair, in a humiliating pose, and thus exposed to everyone's eyes in the wan light of the interrogation room. Seeing the surgical instruments, she had a spasm and let go a thin dribble of urine, which added to her humiliation. For his part, Pierre did his best to hide any sign of emotion.

'What does 'Phoenix' mean?'

Pierre ignored the question. A Gestapo agent picked up a pair of pliers and moved towards Gaëlle, who squirmed on her chair, weeping.

'Where is Louise Desfontaines?' Heindrich asked coldly.

Pierre remained silent, and the torturer closed his pliers on Gaëlle's finger.

'Stop!' she cried.

Louise

On leaving the station, Louise had put Suzy in a cycle-taxi and given the driver the address of the Institute for the Blind. She preferred to walk alone, even if it was a long way to Duroc. She felt an absolute need to walk through the streets to calm the tempest that was raging in her head.

Louise wasn't sure she wanted to continue the mission. The news of her pregnancy had blown to shreds all her certainties, and especially her desire to sacrifice herself. She didn't believe in God, but for the first time she told herself that providence was speaking to her. Going down towards the place de la Concorde, she thought about the last time she and Claude had made love, the night before the operation in Bourg-en-Bresse. The baby must have been conceived that night. And the child that was growing in her belly reminded her of her husband. She had to give him his chance, even if the world collapsed around her, and perhaps precisely because it was collapsing.

But in making the child her priority, Louise was aware that she was putting the mission in danger. Could Jeanne, Suzy and Gaëlle go on without her? Maria was at least as qualified as she was to direct the operation. And then Louise didn't know if she would ever see Pierre alive again.

Giving up the mission meant choosing life, which was stronger than all the dead she had already left behind her, without considering those who were still to fall. So what should she do with the SOE's valise? That money was indispensable for the success of the operation; Maria would need it to ensure the team's escape. Disappearing with the valise was tantamount to condemning them all to death. But without money, Louise couldn't leave France and give birth to her child. She hesitated: using the money amounted to stealing from her own camp and turning her back on her principles. She knew that she was simply incapable of doing that.

She'd been wandering around between Saint Lazare and the place de la Concorde for more than an hour, turning over her thoughts, when she saw a patrol checking passersby at the end of the street. She turned off and went into a square, where she hid behind a tree to watch the soldiers. They searched three more people before heading back to the station. Louise was getting ready to go when she noticed a young woman sitting on a bench and nursing her baby. Contemplating this mother, completely monopolized by the little creature cradled in the crook of her arm, Louise saw a new sign from Claude. He was telling her what to do. She stayed there for more than half an hour, watching the young woman. Finally, calm and sure of her decision, she knew that she was going to return the money to Maria and disappear. But at that moment a German officer entered the square. Louise froze. Had she been spotted? Instinctively, she slipped her hand into her pocket and gripped her revolver. But the officer walked by without even looking at her and went directly up to the woman on the bench. He gave her a kiss and took the baby in his arms and lifted it up towards the sky.

With terror, Louise now understood that it was the German officer's baby. Overcome by a dull rage, she was angry with herself for having been touched by this mother, in whom she now saw only a person corrupted by the SS man whom she had taken into her bed. The monster was giving his cap to his child to use as a toy. He had just demolished all the plans for a happy life that Louise had briefly constructed. In a few seconds, hatred, rancour and vengeance once again dwelt in her heart. In the end, Claude was asking her to continue the struggle.

An hour later, Louise was ringing the doorbell at the Institute for the Blind. The directress, an old lady with a shrivelled face, received her, pale with worry.

'I'm late,' Louise said, 'but the postman fell asleep.'

Recognizing the password, Mme Duchemin heaved a sigh of relief. 'Everyone was wondering what had happened to you. Hurry, they're waiting for you.'

She took Louise to the main refectory. Passing through an external gallery that ran along a courtyard planted with trees, Louise saw a teacher giving piano lessons to a few children dressed in grey blouses. The blank eyes of the blind children made them look like zombies.

Louise found Jeanne and Maria sitting at a table, while Suzy, dressed like a loose woman, was putting the last touches to her makeup.

Maria rolled her eyes. 'We were worried; we thought you'd had a problem.'

'I got lost in the neighbourhood,' Louise lied. 'Isn't Gaëlle here?'

'Not yet, no. She was behind me as I went through the check-point,' Jeanne said. 'Afterwards I lost sight of her.'

Louise glanced at Suzy, who was still powdering her face.

'Suzy, are you going to tell me what you're doing in that get-up?'

'I'd like to know that myself,' Suzy retorted. 'But it seems that it's top secret.'

'I'm taking her to meet someone,' Maria said.

'But you promise me that it's not a German, right?' Suzy asked, suddenly terrified.

Maria didn't answer. Louise immediately reacted: 'Maria, can I speak with you for a minute?'

'Not now, we're in too much of a hurry.'

'Then Suzy isn't going anywhere. She's staying here.'

Seeing that Louise would not yield, and that the others were supporting her, Maria asked Louise to follow her. Jeanne, who didn't appreciate being left out, shouted at them in rage, 'What about us, we just stay here? What's going on? Do we look like half-wits?'

Maria took Louise into the prayer chapel. There, she told Louise where she was taking Suzy. Louise reflected for a moment. Maria went up to a large wardrobe and opened its doors, pushing aside the stoles hanging in it.

'And this Eddy is reliable?' Louise finally asked.

'We've been watching him for some time. Heindrich pays him to find doubles for Suzy. But he's never completely satisfied with the results. I've got him to arrange a meeting between Heindrich and Suzy.' Maria removed the false back of the wardrobe, revealing a hiding-place with weapons and a radio.

'Where is this meeting supposed to take place?'

'Their little love-nest in room 813 at the Regina.'

'And who will pull the trigger?'

'Suzy... We'll have hidden a pistol under the mattress in the room,' Maria said, holding up a pistol.

Louise shook her head. 'Suzy kill Heindrich? She couldn't harm a fly.'

'Then it will be up to you to persuade her to do it.'

'Persuade Suzy to accept a suicide mission? You don't know her.'

Maria looked at her watch. They had to leave; Eddy was waiting for them. While Maria went back to the refectory to get Suzy, Louise sat down on a bench, discouraged. A few seconds later, she saw that Jeanne had come into the room and taken one of the pistols out of the arsenal.

'They've left. What are we going to do in the meantime?'

'We wait,' Louise replied.

Jeanne was amusing herself by pretending to point her weapon at an imaginary enemy. Not knowing whether the pistol was loaded, Louise was on her guard, ready to react.

'In the bus on the way here there was a Boche sitting in front of me,' Jeanne went on. 'Just imagine, he'd left his rifle case open and hadn't even noticed, the bastard... But nothing happened.'

'What should have happened?'

Jeanne stiffened for a moment, gazing into space. Louise suddenly saw a striking resemblance between her and the blind children she'd seen in the courtyard.

'Sometimes it seems to me that the war will be won when we've got the balls to take the rifle off a guy like that and blow his brains out in front of everybody.' A noise made them start. 'Do you think it's Gaëlle?'

Louise shook her head and told Jeanne to be quiet. She knew where she'd heard this low rumbling before: two months earlier, at the station in Bourg-en-Bresse, just before the German column arrived. Carefully, she cracked the door giving onto the courtyard.

She immediately saw a detachment of soldiers coming along the outside gallery. Heindrich was in the lead, followed by two dogs on leashes.

Louise closed the door. 'We're getting out of here – help me, quick!' The two of them grabbed the valises and filled them with weapons.

'What about Gaëlle?' Jeanne asked, seizing a Sten submachine-gun.

'It's too late, we can't wait any longer.'

Mme Duchemin burst into the chapel. 'Come with me, we have to hurry.'

Louise and Jeanne followed her, each carrying a valise.

In the courtyard, at Heindrich's command, two monitors were having the blind children line up. Louise, Jeanne and the directress slipped by and went down the stairs to the cellar. Once there, the directress opened a trap door leading to a dim passageway.

'Go on through the sewers and you'll get to the metro station.' Louise and Jeanne disappeared into the darkness.

'Your brother, did he know that we were at the Institute?'

'He didn't give us up, I know my brother. He would die before he'd talk.'

'Well, if it wasn't him, it must have been Gaëlle…'

Heindrich had searched the prayer chapel and found the arsenal hidden in the wardrobe. Mme Duchemin was immediately brought before the colonel.

'Is that the kind of instruction you provide for your pupils, Madame?' He showed her the pistol, a model used by the British army. The directress lowered her eyes. Two soldiers came in with a terrified blind child, whom they forced to kneel.

'Where is Louise Desfontaines?' Heindrich continued, cocking his pistol.

Mme Duchemin was now weeping. Across from her, her young charge was struggling and calling for help.

'I asked you a question,' Heindrich said.

'I don't know anyone by that name,' the old lady replied.

Heindrich pulled the trigger twice. The child collapsed, hit in the heart by two bullets. Heindrich repeated his question. Panting, but more determined than ever, the directress mumbled that she didn't know any Louise Desfontaines.

When they emerged from the sewers, Jeanne and Louise had no choice but to rejoin Maria and Suzy to warn them not to return to the Institute. Maria had given them the address for their rendez-vous. At nightfall, they arrived in front of a private house at the foot of the Eiffel Tower, in the rue Élisée-Reclus.

'Well, he's doing pretty well for himself, your Eddy,' Jeanne murmured as they passed through the heavy forged-iron gate. 'What does he do for a living?'

'He's a collabo,' Louise answered drily. She put her hand in her coat pocket, feeling for the pistol she'd managed to take from the Institute. Touching the cold metal with her fingers reassured her. Her hand, almost relaxed, closed on the handle and she put her index finger on the trigger. If something should go wrong, she was ready. They got into the lift, and Jeanne pushed the button for the seventh floor.

Eddy poured himself another glass of wine. On the radio, they were playing a song by Yves Montand. 'I love that guy's voice. You'd think someone was tickling him as he sings. I don't like sad singers, they depress me.'

Sitting at the table next to Suzy, Maria gave him her best smile. 'I like him too, and also he's Italian, like me.'

'Yves Montand, Italian? You're kidding me.' He drained his glass and came to sit down with them. Across from him, Suzy was squirming on her chair. She still hadn't said a word since they'd arrived. Eddy looked her straight in the eyes.

'It's smashing, isn't it Suzy? Thanks to you, I'm going to finally be able to do business with the Colonel again.'

'What colonel?' Suzy asked.

Eddy paused. Seeing the worried look that Suzy gave Maria, he realized that she didn't know all the details. 'Well, the one I'm going to introduce you to tomorrow. Here, let me show you something – you'll understand.'

He got up and staggered towards a bureau. He opened a drawer and took out a photo. 'Look at that, I'm not making it up. You're the very image of the girl that he's been after for more than two years. It's as if heaven had sent you.' He handed Suzy the picture in which Liliane was posing in her Chanel dress with her lover on the evening that had marked the zenith of her affair with Karl. Suzy could not hide her shock.

At that moment, someone knocked at the door. Maria turned to Eddy. 'Are you expecting someone?'

'No, I can't imagine who it could be,' Eddy murmured, heading for the door. Maria glanced at her bag and the pistol that was in it. Opposite her, Suzy was staring at her darkly.

'Good evening, ladies, can I do something for you?' Eddy had opened the door part way to find Louise and Jeanne, who hadn't expected to see such a boyish fellow. Louise relaxed and took her finger off the trigger of the pistol in her pocket.

'Sorry to disturb you, but we're friends of Maria and her cousin Suzy...I've got something to tell them.'

Eddy opened the door wide and invited them to come in. 'Welcome, then. Friends of my friends are my friends, and even more when they're as pretty as you are.'

Louise thanked him and walked into the vestibule, still carrying Buck's valise in her hand. The apartment was sumptuous, and richly decorated with artworks, most of them from abroad. This Eddy knew how to play his cards. As Louise had asked, Jeanne pretended to be delighted with every knick-knack, every ceiling moulding. 'A beautiful place you've got here... Congratulations...' Seeing them come in, Maria put her pistol back in her bag. Suzy looked daggers at both of them, and her hands began to tremble slightly.

'There was a raid at the Institute,' Louise murmured.

'I know,' Maria replied. 'We saw the Germans as we were leaving.'

Suzy stood up. 'You want to put me back in Heindrich's bed, is that it? You've really taken me for a ride! What a bunch of shits! Pierre, you, Buck, the whole SOE!' she screamed at Louise.

Eddy, who had just come back into the room with Jeanne, stunned, turned to Maria: 'The SOE? What's your cousin talking about?'

With a cry of rage, Suzy tore up the photo.

'Hey, you can't do that! That's my photo,' Eddy moaned, trying to stop her.

'I'll never see Karl again, do you hear me? I'd rather die! Right here and now! You'll have to take my dead body into his bedroom. And here's my shroud!' She yanked the tablecloth, sending the dishes flying.

'What's got into her? Why is she talking about Heindrich?' Eddy asked, completely at sea.

Jeanne didn't give him time to think, using the butt of her pistol to knock him to the floor with a violent blow to the back of the neck. Not hard enough, she thought, because he was still moving and moaning. She turned the pistol around and was about to hit him in the face with the barrel when Louise stopped her. 'We're going to stay here. Help me tie him up.'

As they tied Eddy's hands with a curtain cord, Maria took her crystal radio out of her valise and set it up. 'I'm going to tell Buck about the raid.'

They suddenly heard the sound of glass breaking at the end of the hallway. Louise and Jeanne looked at each other: 'Suzy!' They ran to the bedroom and found Suzy with her back to the wall, a shard of glass held to her wrist.

'No one is going to force me to see him again, do you hear?'

'Calm down. We just want to talk,' Louise said, holding out her hand.

'Don't come any closer or I'll kill myself, I swear I will!' The shard's point was now pushed hard against her skin. Suzy was trembling more and more, and her eyes were filled with tears. Louise realized that she had reached the end of her tether. 'I don't want to talk any more, I don't want to talk about all that. Have you still not understood?'

Jeanne moved towards her in a friendly way, smiling. 'You're not going to kill yourself over a guy, are you? Not over a Nazi, at least.'

'I wasn't with a Nazi, I was in love with a German; it's not the same thing, but you don't understand anything.' Suzy threw away the shard of glass and grabbed a bottle of cognac on the mantlepiece staring at the floor and breathing heavily. Jeanne patted her shoulder.

'Of course we understand, you just need to explain it to us.'

'All we're asking of you,' Louise continued, 'is to have a short conversation with him. Two minutes at most. Jeanne and I will take care of the rest.'

Suzy continued to look down at the floor. Louise lifted her chin and looked her straight in the eyes. 'You can't let us down. We really need you.'

Suzy made a great effort to look back at her, and then collapsed in her arms, wracked by sobs. Louise was surprised to find herself hugging her tightly, as if the better to console her.

Jeanne seized the bottle and finished it off.

A few minutes later, things were quiet again in the big apartment. Still hunched over her radio, the headset clamped over her hair, Maria was continuing to transmit her message. Behind her, Louise was waiting, her arms crossed.

'Not too tired?'

Maria smiled at her. 'When I saw the Germans coming, I thought you and I would never see each other again.'

'It wasn't my time, that's all,' Louise replied.

'Do you believe in that stuff?'

'I think that nothing ever happens by chance.'

The two women looked at each other for a long time without saying anything. Although the window was open, no sound came up from the street, which seemed dead. Louise could no longer bear the silence of curfews; she didn't like those calm nights, she wanted music, the shouts of drunks, everything that makes up life in peacetime.

'It's always at times like this that I have gloomy thoughts,' Maria murmured. 'I feel my ghosts all around me.'

'Are you talking about your family?' Louise asked.

Maria nodded. 'I think there may still be one who's alive … and it's for him that I'm fighting.' Her words found an echo in Louise. She went up to her friend and took her in her arms.

'You're right, we have to fight for the living.'

In the next room, Jeanne opened the door of a closet in which Eddy had just regained consciousness. Trussed up like a chicken, he could only roll his eyes and kick the wall with his feet, and he was doing just that. 'If you keep that up, I'm going to put your lights out, you understand?' Jeanne grumbled. He stopped moving, and breathed more slowly. Closing the door, Jeanne saw Suzy lying on the sofa. She was lighting a cigarette.

'We were supposed to get married at Saint-Germain-des-Prés,' Suzy began. 'He'd given me a magnificent dress. By Chanel, you know?'

'I haven't followed fashions much recently, you'll have to excuse me.'

'Karl joined the Hitler Youth because it was the only way he could get an education and enter the military academy. He comes from a very humble background and didn't want to end up like his parents.'

'That's right … He became a Nazi the way I became a whore, in fact …'

Suzy gave a wounded look.

'So why did you leave him, if life with this Fritz was so great?' Jeanne asked.

'I didn't care whether he was a Nazi or a Maquisard. I was horrified by the idea of belonging to a man. And that's what being married means. It was more than I could stand.'

Jeanne was speechless. She looked at Louise, who'd been standing in the hall, listening to them through the half-open door.

Suzy was overcome again by a wave of emotion, and began weeping again.

'Come on, it's not so bad as all that. In the end, you did what you had to, even if it wasn't for the right reasons.'

Suzy turned towards her and hesitated, as if about to confess something important. 'I never knew that I was carrying his child.'

Louise instinctively put her hand on her belly. Confused and not knowing what to say, Jeanne looked at Suzy as if she were seeing her for the first time. 'You've got a child? You?'

Suzy shook her head. 'I could never have been married, and then a mother, can you imagine?'

'You did away with it?'

Suzy didn't answer. Jeanne was hanging on her every word now, as if her confession had touched her deeply. But Suzy couldn't say any more. She looked at the wall to hide her tears, which were flowing more than ever. Jeanne handed her a handkerchief.

'You abandoned it, that's it?'

'He was placed with a family in Liverpool. His Nazi father and his collaborator mother are forgotten. It'll be much better for him … Now you know who you're dealing with.' Suzy rose and shut herself up in the lavatory. She locked the door and broke into tears.

Louise entered the room and sat down on the sofa. She looked at her watch. 'Still no answer from London?'

'Seven minutes more, and then we turn it off,' Maria said. No point in letting themselves be located.

'Do you want some coffee while we wait?' Jeanne asked.

'Real coffee?'

'Hundred per cent black market.'

They went into the huge kitchen. Jeanne poured the coffee into porcelain cups she'd found in a buffet. Louise examined the room: the apartment was extremely luxurious, and completely unlike Eddy, whose taste in matters of crockery and decoration seemed extremely limited.

'I'm sure Suzy is tormented by having done that to her kid,' Jeanne said.

Since Suzy had made her confession, Jeanne felt even more concerned. Something in this story touched her deeply, but Louise didn't go so far as to ask her to explain. Even if she knew a great deal about the members of her team, she respected their private aspects.

'She would probably have been a poor mother. Even certainly.'

'How can you say that,' Jeanne asked. 'If he's not dead, the worst thing in the world happened to that kid.'

'There's always something worse, you know.'

'You don't believe in pity, is that it? Try to be a little more human, for once.'

'This morning, in the train, I learned that I've been pregnant for three months. I can't be more human than that.'

Jeanne was stunned by this news.

'We'd been trying to have a child for two years,' Louise added with bitter irony.

'But then … you're … you're going to stop the mission?'

'I thought about it. And then I said to myself that I didn't want to give birth in a world like this.'

Jeanne took Louise's hand. For the first time in their odyssey, she showed her a real mark of affection. They remained quiet until they suddenly heard Maria cry out in the office next door, 'Here it is! London is answering!'

Louise and Jeanne rushed to join her. The headset lying on the table, she was deciphering the message as it came in.

'Well?' Louise asked impatiently. Maria finished writing. She turned to Louise.

'Buck is asking you to make contact with a certain Melchior, tomorrow morning, in the Jardin des Plantes. He will give you instructions. The rendezvous is set for ten-thirty a.m. in the Main Gallery of Evolution.'

Louise had always been afraid of false messages sent by the Germans, and she arrived half an hour early to scope out the surroundings. This time, everything seemed normal. She sat down on a bench outside the building and tried to clear her mind. She'd passed a very agitated night, thinking constantly about Claude. She'd never felt him so present. She saw him everywhere, and during the night she could have sworn she'd heard him whispering unintelligible words in her ear. Was it a harbinger of her death? Like Maria, she dragged her ghosts around with her, and they now included, perhaps, Pierre and Gaëlle. Louise decided to remain deaf to their calls. Once again, she was fighting for the living, and for them alone.

In the middle of the gallery, a tall, dark-haired man wearing small round spectacles was leafing through a museum catalogue. He wore a royal-blue shirt, and corresponded to the description Maria had given. Louise decided to go up to him.

'The elephant has broken a tusk,' she said in a low voice.

The man looked up from his catalogue. After glancing furtively right and left, he gave her a sign to follow him to the storeroom. Louise suddenly felt ill at ease amid all these stuffed animals.

'The operation will take place at noon, on the platform at the Concorde metro station.'

'What? Is Buck sending us to pick up Gaëlle? She denounced us.'

'Colonel Buckmaster is certain that Heindrich will be at the rendezvous. You are to kill him.'

'I beg your pardon? In the metro, out in the open?'

'It's less risky than at the Regina.'

'What about Suzy, don't you trust her any more?'

'Only to set the trap. As for the rest, Buck prefers to rely on you. In the metro you can count on the complicity of the employees. Some of them belong to our network.'

Melchior unwrapped a package he'd put on the table. In it was a rifle with a telescopic sight. Suddenly apprehensive, Louise realized that she hadn't used one of those since the operation in Bourg-en-Bresse. Without showing her emotion, she examined the weapon closely, fitting the stock to her shoulder and checking the sight.

'I got it last night,' Melchior continued. 'Will it work for you?'

Louise nodded and put the rifle back on the table. Melchior took out a leather bag and laid it in front of her. 'I found this bag that you can use to carry the rifle. Is it all right?'

Without answering, Louise began disassembling the rifle to put it in the bag. 'About my brother ... Do you have any news?'

'He's alive, that's all we know.'

'Does he have any chance of escaping?'

Melchior shook his head, depriving Louise of all hope. The rifle was now completely disassembled and stored at the bottom of the bag. 'I know what you're thinking about,' he said. 'But the colonel doesn't want you to put the operation in danger by trying to save your brother.'

'I've always completed the missions I've been assigned. And I'll do everything I can to prevent my brother from being decapitated as a spy.' She picked up the bag and left the storeroom without looking at Melchior again.

At the door to the lift, just as she was about to enter Eddy's place, Louise heard cries coming from the apartment. Holding her pistol, she burst into the room and found Jeanne with a pistol in her hand, threatening a young man, while Suzy, furious, was hitting him with her fists. Maria stood back, ready to fire if necessary.

'I'm going to kill this scum, it'll calm me down,' Jeanne screamed, nearly out of her mind.

Louise intervened. 'What's wrong with you? Are you ill?'

'This piece of garbage took over the apartment of a Jewish family,' Jeanne bellowed. 'Look what we found in the closets!' Suzy showed Louise a child's coat with a yellow star sewn onto it.

Eddy tried to justify himself. 'The apartment was empty, they gave it to me. I can't help it if someone pulled strings for me!'

'My whole family was deported,' Maria said. 'I don't know what's keeping me from killing you right here.'

'What's holding you back is that we still need him,' Louise replied, pushing Jeanne's pistol away.

'Need me for what?'

'If you're thinking about informing on us, I'll bring you quickly up to date. Have you heard about the Allied offensive?'

Eddy was speechless. All eyes were on him, as well as Maria's pistol.

'To make conversation, people do talk about it. But I haven't yet seen any sign of it.'

'Go ahead, try and be clever,' Jeanne shouted. 'Soon there won't be a single Boche in Paris!'

Eddy shrugged. 'That won't change anything for a guy like me.'

'You think so? I'm not so sure,' Louise answered. 'There'll always be someone who remembers that you lived here. And then ...'

Worried, Eddy stared at her.

'We're giving you a chance to redeem yourself, as clean as a new penny,' Louise added.

'And if I help you out, you'll put in a word for me with the Rosbifs, is that it?'

'You began the war by working for the Germans, you'll end it working for the English. In the end, there'll be no one more French than you.'

Eddy's face hardened again. He still wasn't convinced. 'And if I refuse? You're going to kill me?'

Louise gave Maria a look to tell her to open the SOE's valise. All lined up like soldiers on parade, the bundles of bills appeared before Eddy's dazed eyes.

'Better yet. You'll have to explain to the Gestapo how you inherited such a lot of money.'

'Especially when they find out that it came from England,' Maria said.

With a forced smile, Eddy accepted their conditions.

Gaëlle

The night seemed endless. Handcuffed and crouched in a garret of the Gestapo building, Gaëlle could not sleep, despite the fatigue that overwhelmed her. Her finger hurt terribly, and the bandage covering it didn't help. The interrogation still haunted her. She felt ashamed to have talked so easily, ashamed to have been afraid of pain. As soon as she'd felt her nail being detached, she hadn't been able to stop herself shouting, 'The Duroc Institute for the Blind! That's where we were supposed to meet and receive orders for a new mission!'

Since then, the Nazi officer's eyes had been tormenting her. The light she'd seen in them had ultimately been worse than the torture. Pierre's reaction gnawed at her as well: a mixture of stupefaction, scorn and pity.

How many hours had gone by since she confessed? She couldn't have said. She'd lost all idea of time long ago. But she was sure of one thing: Louise, Maria, Jeanne and Suzy had now all been arrested. Because of her. She would never forgive herself.

'Your cyanide pill? Do you still have it?' Pierre murmured.

Gaëlle didn't move. Chained to the same pipe, they hadn't exchanged a single word since they'd been locked up. She felt incapable of confronting him.

'Have you got it on you? Answer me, damn it!'

'I'm afraid... Do you know what that means?'

Suddenly Pierre grabbed Gaëlle by the neck, putting one hand on her mouth to keep her from crying out, using the other to choke her. Her eyes bulging, Gaëlle struggled and made muffled cries. A few more seconds and her brain would lack oxygen, and it would be over.

The door of the cell opened, and two German soldiers started shouting. One of them struck Pierre violently in the face with the butt of his rifle, making him let go. Freed, Gaëlle was still petrified with fear and panting like a fish out of water. As the soldiers unchained Pierre and dragged him out of the cell, Heindrich came into the garret. Seeing Gaëlle's flushed face, he looked sad.

'Using such fragile women...your Mr Buckmaster disappoints me.' He offered Gaëlle a handkerchief to dry her tears, but she refused it. Then he crouched down to wipe her face with a gentleness that astonished her. 'I'm going to need your help again. I almost caught your friends at the Institute...' Gaëlle tried to conceal her relief. 'When and where are you supposed to be picked up?'

'Picked up?'

'Don't pretend you don't know what I'm talking about. I know how the SOE operates...'

Gaëlle looked straight at Heindrich. He was a mystery to her. He was cruel, but had a benevolent voice. He was determined, but there was something broken in his eyes. He had taken no pleasure in seeing her tortured, but neither had he shown any mercy. She knew that he would have her tortured again if he had to.

'Louise knows now that I betrayed them. She will never go to the rendezvous.'

'Louise likes to take risks.'

Secretly, Gaëlle thought Heindrich was right about that. He'd seen Louise only once, but he seemed to know so her well. 'If I talk, what will you give me in return?' she said.

'Your freedom.'

'Freedom to be judged and condemned by the SOE?' She stifled the nosebleed that his words had provoked. 'What time is it?' she asked.

Heindrich looked at his watch. 'ten-forty… Why?'

'It's at noon. Concorde metro station, direction Pont-de-Neuilly, on the platform.'

Heindrich gave commands; he wanted Gaëlle to look exactly as she did when she got off the train at Saint Lazare. Since her clothes had been torn during her interrogation, Heindrich ordered a seamstress to repair her blouse and skirt. Gaëlle's face also had to be heavily made up to conceal the marks left by the blows she'd received. The colonel wanted her to look as if she'd spent the night in a hotel without having had the time to do herself up before leaving. To hide the fingernail that had been torn off, Gaëlle was told to keep her hands in her pockets. While the seamstress was finishing her repairs, Gaëlle closed her eyes and began to pray under her breath.

Two Gestapo agents took her to a taxi parked in the courtyard. One of the men took the wheel while Gaëlle got in the back seat with the other. The taxi went up avenue Foch, round the Arc de Triomphe, and then down the Champs-Élysées to the place de la Concorde. Gaëlle hadn't been in Paris for years. She remembered the City of Light as a noisy capital with boulevards crowded with tourists. The sight of empty shops and the great avenues now deserted, and lined with signs written in German, depressed her.

Heindrich had taken every precaution. He was afraid Louise would be suspicious, and would be keeping an eye on Gaëlle. The taxi stopped near the metro station. Gaëlle immediately spotted the two Gestapo agents who were waiting for her at the top of the stairs, pretending to be deep in conversation. She ignored them and went down the stairway into the station. The two men followed her. In the underground tunnel, a Parisienne with a familiar walk passed by her. Without turning her head towards Gaëlle, Jeanne whispered, 'Louise's order: once you're on the platform, don't move, even if there's a ruckus…' Then she turned in another direction as if nothing had happened.

Gaëlle handed her ticket to the ticket-puncher, and went onto the platform, where about a dozen people were waiting. But she didn't see Louise. Sitting down on a bench near the stationmaster's booth, she caught sight of the two men who were following her. At the other end of the platform, two additional agents had positioned themselves to block the exit. There were thus four of them in all, not counting those she hadn't spotted and who might be waiting among the other passengers alongside her. Gaëlle examined her neighbours one by one. Six men and four women. No children, thank God. But their faces didn't betray their intentions. Why had Jeanne suggested that there might be a ruckus? What did Louise have in mind?

Then Gaëlle heard the click of high heels; a woman was coming. Like the Gestapo agents, Gaëlle looked towards the entrance to the platform. Maria had just appeared, wearing a light tan coat. She handed her ticket to the ticket-puncher, who nodded discreetly towards the stationmaster's booth. Coolly, Maria walked down the platform without addressing the slightest sign to Gaëlle, who still didn't understand what was going on. The Gestapo men, who didn't have a description of Maria, relaxed as Jeanne also arrived. Using all her charm, she asked one of the men for a light, and then went to sit down not far from Maria.

Her hands still in her pockets, Gaëlle felt her palms getting increasingly damp. She no longer doubted that something was going to happen. Maria and Jeanne had no reason to come together to pick her up. And why had the ticket-puncher indicated the stationmaster's box to Maria? Gaëlle's heart was beating wildly. On her left, a train was arriving. She took advantage of this to look towards Maria and Jeanne, who'd just stood up.

The train came into the station. The doors opened to release a flood of passengers, which Jeanne joined in order to reach the end of the platform, near the tunnel. Maria got on the train. Looking at her expectantly, the two agents' eyes were asking Gaëlle where Louise was. That was when the telephone at the head of the platform began to ring, forcing the driver to get out of the engine. After a brief conversation, he hung up the receiver and addressed the passengers: 'Ladies and gentlemen, I am informed that an incident has occurred at Champs-Élysées-Clemenceau station. I am waiting for a green light before leaving.'

Gaëlle's heart almost stopped. She was sure that this was a signal. Furthermore, on her right Jeanne was still facing the tunnel. In the silent station, the sound of footfalls came from the stairway. Gaëlle held her breath: Suzy had just appeared on the opposite platform. A young man wearing a dark grey suit and a cap came to meet her. Gaëlle realized that she was paying too much attention to them. She had to adhere to the letter of the order Jeanne had transmitted, and keep looking indifferent. As another train was coming into the station on Suzy's side of the tracks, Gaëlle scanned the train that was already in. Its doors were still wide open. Maria, sitting near a window, remained perfectly calm, and did not look at Suzy and her escort as they boarded the second train and sat down together.

Gaëlle suddenly noticed a silhouette coming out of the station-master's booth. It was Heindrich, wearing a flannel suit. He was staring, hypnotized, at the opposite platform. Then she realized that he'd seen Suzy. Heindrich, completely oblivious to what was going on around him, got into the train, which was still sitting at the platform, and called out, 'Liliane!' Gaëlle could see Suzy's face peeking over the young man's shoulder. She'd gone pale, and Heindrich was trying to break the windowpane in order to talk to her. Gaëlle saw Maria get up and take a pistol out of her bag. Heindrich, completely absorbed in Suzy, paid her no attention. Maria was pointing her pistol at the colonel's back. At the same moment, deafening reports were heard. Before dropping to the floor, Gaëlle just had time to see another soldier emerge from the booth. He had just fired, and his bullets had shattered the carriage's window and hit Maria in her left side. Inside the carriage, all the passengers had thrown themselves to the floor, screaming. With a horrified grimace, Heindrich turned to fire at the Italian woman, emptying his magazine into her. In the carriage opposite, Suzy was holding her head in her hands and watching Maria's body jerk like an out-of-control marionette.

On the platform, a Gestapo agent pinned Gaëlle to the floor and handcuffed her. That was when she saw her in the tunnel, briefly illuminated by the flash of gunfire. Louise. In position on the tracks, a rifle with a telescopic sight at her shoulder, she was waiting for Heindrich to step back onto the platform.

Gaëlle summoned all her strength and shouted as loudly as she could, 'It's a trap, Louise! Run!'

Heindrich

Karl stared at Maria's face. On it was the expression of those who have been overtaken by death without having been prepared to meet it. If Volker hadn't reacted in time, he would have been the one wearing this death-mask, who would have been riddled with bullets, slumped on a banquette with his arms thrown wide, and he couldn't get that idea out of his head.

God was giving him another sign. His time had not come. So long as he had not completed his mission, he would be invulnerable. He was now convinced of this.

The train on the other side started up. He saw it moving away carrying a terrified Liliane, who was screaming as she clutched Eddy.

He hadn't dreamed it. He'd seen Liliane. Not a double, but the real Liliane this time. He couldn't think it was just chance.

The Gestapo agents made all the passengers exit the carriages and line up on the platform. Heindrich rushed over to the ticket-puncher and pulled him into the booth. 'Tell the train that has just left to stop,' he ordered, handing the man the telephone.

'It's impossible to do that when it's between stations.'

Heindrich put the barrel of his pistol to the man's temple. Resigned, the ticket-puncher took the receiver. 'Hello – this is Bartier, at Concorde. Stop the train heading for Château-de-Vincennes…' He paused and then, terrified, told the officer, 'It's too late, it's already at the Tuileries.'

Furious, Heindrich left the booth to inspect the civilians lined up on the platform, holding their hands up like prisoners. How many of them were involved in the operation? He examined one woman a few metres away from him; it seemed to him that he'd seen her somewhere before. He stopped himself – he was so upset that he was suspicious of all the passengers.

Still crouching in the tunnel, Louise saw Heindrich move right into her line of fire, with Jeanne alongside him, her eyes lowered. It was now or never. The headlight of the next train suddenly illumined the tunnel behind her. She paid no attention, putting one knee on the ground to take aim. The train was approaching. Seeing her on the tracks, the driver sounded his horn.

On the platform, Heindrich heard the horn. Just as he turned towards the tunnel, a flash lit up the dark and he felt a lancing pain in his ear. Blood spurted onto his hands. His men opened fire in the direction of the tunnel. Their bullets hit the engine's headlights, which exploded. Taking advantage of the general panic, Jeanne got to the exit, where an agent blocked her way. Clutching him, she plunged a knife into his stomach and went on her way.

As the Germans were shooting at her, Louise had taken refuge in a niche in the tunnel, where she let the train go by. She knew that she'd missed Heindrich, and threw down her rifle in rage. With a pistol in her hand, she escaped by an iron stairway leading to the maintenance area.

Indifferent to his wound, which was still bleeding, Karl ordered the firing to stop, and had a barrier set up at every exit from the station. Louise Desfontaines had fired on him, he was sure of that. His men had her description; she couldn't get away from them. She had failed once again to kill him. The gods were protecting him.

Following the crowd of passengers, Jeanne headed for the rue Royale exit. She saw the agents posted at the top of the steps, holding photos in their hands and scanning the passengers. They can't have a description of me, she thought, otherwise Heindrich would have spotted me on the platform. She started up the stairs with her fists clenched, and went through the barrier without any difficulty. A few metres further on she stopped to gather her wits.

Emerging from a service hatch, Louise also mixed with other passengers and went up the corridor towards the exit. In her pocket, she was still gripping the handle of her pistol, concealing herself as best she could behind two hefty men. The flow of passengers slowed as it approached the exit, and Louise had to stand on tiptoe to see the three agents blocking the way at the top of the stairs. She noticed the photo in the hand of one of the men, turned around and stopped dead when she saw Heindrich and the Gestapo men appear at the end of the corridor. Caught in the middle, she preferred the barrier, no matter what the cost.

Then everything happened as if in a bad dream. Her finger on the trigger, she came up to the three agents. On seeing the look given her by the tallest one, she realized that he'd recognized her. She had no time to draw her pistol; behind her, two men seized her, threw her to the ground, and handcuffed her. Louise closed her eyes; she would have preferred to die on the steps of this station, where a fine drizzle was starting to fall. The two men stood her up, and she saw Heindrich's blood-stained face looking at her. Holding his hand to his ragged ear, he seemed as shocked as she was, but did not express the slightest emotion. He just nodded, and Louise felt herself lifted off the ground by two Gestapo men who carried her towards a car. Before being thrown into the vehicle, in which Gaëlle was already sitting, she had time to see Jeanne disappear into the Tuileries garden.

The colonel should have been happy: Louise Desfontaines was his prisoner. But he was thinking only of Liliane. What had she been doing in that station, where an assassination attempt could have cost her her life? Had she really been there by chance? He would have liked to believe that, but his instinct made him wary. On the way back, he examined all the possibilities and was left with only one of them. Eddy had heard about her and had set up a meeting with her. Weren't the simplest explanations always the best? Why did he always feel compelled to complicate everything? Eddy was still trying to track down the perfect double, and he'd finally come across the rare pearl. But then why did he set the rendezvous on that platform at just that time? The coincidences were multiplying, and it wasn't credible; was Eddy in on the operation too? There was only one way to find out.

In one of the Gestapo's offices, a doctor was sewing up Karl's ear while he called the telephone operator to ask for Eddy's number. The phone rang and rang. The cretin wasn't at home. What if Liliane had been wounded in the shooting? Just when he was about to find her again? He was considering that horrible possibility when he heard Eddy's voice.

'Hello?'

'Eddy? What were you doing in the metro a little while ago?'

'Colonel? I didn't recognize your voice.'

'Answer me, Eddy.'

'Excuse me, I'm still all upset... What a business! I almost got hit, you know...'

'Who was with you?'

He could sense the fear in Eddy's voice now.

'What do you mean, Colonel?'

'I saw you on the platform at the Concorde station. Who was that woman who got on the train with you?'

'You were there, too, Colonel? I hope you weren't hit, at least?'

'Stop playing the fool, Eddy, and answer me. Or should I send a patrol to bring you in?'

Eddy paused. Heindrich imagined him terrified, twisting his tie between his fingers. 'Well, I had a meeting with someone who should please you, I think.'

'Where is she?'

'She's not with me any longer, Colonel. She was just passing through Paris. She's leaving soon, I believe.'

'Listen to me, Eddy. You're going to go back and look for her. You will find a way to bring her to me at six this evening, at the Regina, in the usual place.'

'At the Regina? But Colonel...'

'Don't disappoint me, Eddy!' Heindrich hung up.

Eddy stood thunderstruck in the middle of the lounge, the receiver glued to his ear. At his side, Jeanne put down the receiver he'd allowed her to use to listen in on the conversation. Suzy continued to sit immobile on the sofa, staring into space.

'We've got to get out of here,' Eddy said.

'And the mission?' Jeanne replied, getting up.

'Louise is screwed, and the mission too. You do what you want. I'm going to take off.' He went over to the SOE valise and took out a dozen bundles of bills. 'I'm taking my share. After what happened in the metro, I deserve it.'

Jeanne pointed her pistol at him. 'You're not going anywhere, and you're going to put that money down. I don't want Louise to die for nothing. We're going to go all the way.'

'You think so? And can you tell me how we're going to do that?'

'I'll kill him,' Suzy said.

Incredulous, Jeanne and Eddy looked at her. Since the shooting in the metro, a veil had settled over her eyes. She no longer looked like a fearful doe.

'Drive me to the hotel. Arrange for me to be alone with him and I'll kill him.'

Louise

'Louise, please, help me.' Chained to the radiator, Louise heard Gaëlle call to her from the next room. Since they'd arrived at the Gestapo offices, the two women had been held in adjoining rooms, where they'd been stripped of all their clothes except their slips. Louise had nonetheless hung on to her cyanide pill in a tube that she could still feel against her skin inside her bra. That was what Gaëlle was asking for now, she knew it.

'Louise, I'm begging you,' Gaëlle continued. Through the open door between the two rooms, Louise could see her face, so ravaged by suffering as to be unrecognizable. If at first Louise had been angry at Gaëlle for not having killed herself when she should have, she now felt only a profound compassion for her. In fact, she couldn't refuse her a dignified exit. After wriggling about, Louise managed to get her fingers on the little metal tube, from which she extracted the pill. She hesitated one last time, then rolled the pill over the floor. Gaëlle caught it and leaned back against the wall, at peace.

'Do you forgive me?'

Louise was weeping now. Was it the feeling of death being so close? She couldn't have said, but her tears were flowing all by themselves, and she couldn't stop them.

'Tell me that you forgive me,' Gaëlle said again.

Louise turned towards her. 'I forgive you.'

Gaëlle smiled. Louise could hear her praying in a low voice. She murmured for a few seconds, and then there was a long silence. Gaëlle began to cough and breathe irregularly. She started shivering and groaning as she was shaken by increasingly violent convulsions. Her legs pounded the floor with an unbearable sound. Louise stopped her ears and closed her eyes. She waited for what seemed to her an eternity. When it was silent again, she turned around. Gaëlle was lying on the floor, her eyes wide open, finally free.

Her corpse was discovered an hour later. Two guards carried it away, wrapped in a blanket. Gaëlle's arm dragged along the floor for a few metres. That was Louise's last image of her.

'Louise Desfontaines, married name Granville. Sister of Lieutenant Pierre Desfontaines, member of the SOE, arrested by the Gestapo last year at Le Mans. It's always moving to see a family brought together again.' Smiling, Heindrich closed Louise's file.

Pierre was tied to a chair, and looked at Heindrich with empty eyes. Behind him, his sister, her wrists and ankles strapped, was near the bathtub.

'Why did you try twice to kill me, Louise?' Heindrich went on in a soft voice. Louise remained silent, refusing even to look at him. To break her resistance, a henchman gave her a violent slap in the face. Pierre gripped his chair when Heindrich approached him.

'Why was that British geologist so important to the SOE? And what does his message mean?'

A thin rivulet of blood ran out of Louise's nose. She couldn't help looking at the secretary sitting behind her typewriter, ready to type confessions that would never be made.

'Well?' Heindrich asked impatiently.

Pierre said nothing. Infuriated, the colonel gave a sign to the torturers. Pierre closed his eyes as he heard his sister's head being pushed underwater.

Louise held her breath, her eyelids closed. In her mind's eye she saw Gaëlle's inert body, her face calm and at peace. It was so tempting. Why not just let herself go? Why shouldn't she let the water flow into her lungs?

Pierre found it hard to keep his eyes closed. Mentally, he counted: one, two, three... His sister had had her face underwater for more than a minute. Pierre had to take himself out of this room and imagine himself walking down a path in the happy past. For the first time, he couldn't do it.

The henchmen pulled Louise's head out of the water; she was about to suffocate. Heindrich attacked again, holding the photos of the blocks of concrete under Pierre's nose. 'I'm an only son, Monsieur Desfontaines, and I'd like to think that a brother and sister would love each other more than anything. And although I'd have liked to have a sister like Louise, I'd have hated to have a brother like you...'

Pierre walled himself up in his silence. Discouraged, Heindrich signalled to his henchmen again. They grabbed Louise by the hair and lifted her up. She screamed with all her might. Still motionless in front of her typewriter, the secretary didn't even wince.

Louise had her head below water again, and was still struggling. Never had she wanted so much for it all to be over. She was even ready to believe in God if the creator could help her lose consciousness. She implored Claude, Gaëlle and Maria, wherever they were, to come and get her.

Volker came into the room. Hearing Louise's increasingly unbearable screams, he hesitated, then went up to Heindrich and whispered in his ear. 'I've just reached Rommel's secretary. He's supposed to meet his wife in Ulm tomorrow afternoon. He could receive you in Berlin, very briefly, just before he leaves…'

'I've still got to have something to tell him,' Heindrich replied, disillusioned. Louise's cries were becoming less intense. Pierre looked like he was about to crack. Heindrich looked at him fixedly. 'She won't hold out for long. You're the only one who can still save her.'

For the first time, Pierre looked him straight in the eyes. 'If I talk, do I have your word that you'll let her live?'

Heindrich shook Pierre's hand. 'You have my word as a man.'

'I want your word as an officer.'

Heindrich had Louise's head taken out of the water. She was no longer choking, and she was no longer screaming. Panicked, the colonel examined her personally. When he felt her pulse beating feebly, he calmed down.

Wrapped in a blanket, Louise slowly came round. The lighting in the room seemed dimmer. She heard her brother's voice whispering unintelligible words to Heindrich. The secretary asked him to speak up because she couldn't hear him.

'The blocks…are supposed to be towed by a boat…' Pierre began.

Heindrich frowned. Behind him, the typewriter clattered. 'Wait a minute. Are you telling me that these concrete cubes are supposed to travel across the Channel? How?'

'Floating,' Pierre answered.

'You mean they're hollow?'

Pierre nodded. 'As they near the coast, they'll be filled with water and sunk near the beaches.'

'Why?'

Pierre hesitated. He knew that he'd arrived at the point of no return. Louise was looking at him, weak, dripping, and totally alarmed. She couldn't believe her ears.

'Don't talk, Pierre. I'm begging you, don't!' she managed to say.

Louise was struck a blow to the belly so powerful that it stretched her out on the floor, where she received a volley of kicks. She tried to protect her stomach, but an intense pain was already shooting through her. 'No!' she shouted. 'I beg you!'

'Stop!' Heindrich ordered.

Louise remained prostrate on the floor, her arms wrapped around her belly. She was now trembling.

'Why sink them near the beaches? Go on, speak!'

'To construct a floating port by connecting them together with gangways.'

Heindrich froze. Pierre hung his head; he could no longer bear Heindrich's gaze. The colonel reflected on what he'd learned, and realized its significance. After the failed attempt at Dieppe, this was the Americans' only chance to land on a beach in Normandy. And their purpose was to invade France.

He turned to Volker. A dazed look on his face, he told Volker in German, 'We're going to the Regina. You will call Rommel from there. Tell him I'll be in Berlin.'

'You know him better than I do,' Volker replied. 'A private conversation won't be enough – he'll want proof. You'll have to take the prisoner with you, I don't see any other solution.'

'Arrange that for me. I'll take the night train and see him at the first opportunity.' Volker clicked his heels together and saluted the colonel.

Heindrich looked at Louise and Pierre with a smile. 'I'll keep my promise, Monsieur Desfontaines. Your sister will live.' And he left the room.

Louise and Pierre looked at each other in silence. In her brother's eyes, she could see his shame at having talked. In hers, he saw for the first time all the love mixed with compassion that she had for him.

The network headed by Melchior had agents even in the corridors of the Hotel Regina. When Heindrich and Volker crossed the great lobby to enter their offices, the agent posted at the reception desk kept an eye on them. He was well acquainted with these two men. Their rapid steps and excited faces told him that something unusual was happening. He soon intercepted Volker's telephone call asking to speak to Field Marshal Rommel's aide-de-camp. The receptionist discreetly took down the conversation. A few minutes later, Melchior received the message in his office at the National Museum of Natural History and immediately informed London. Less than two hours after Volker's call, Buckmaster and his staff knew that Heindrich was planning to go to Berlin with Pierre Desfontaines. They were to take the train at 10.37 that evening, and would meet Rommel on the morning of 4 June. The reasons for this meeting remained vague, but everything indicated that Pierre had talked. When Churchill was informed of this, he thought it too late to change the plans; bad weather had already caused the landing to be delayed until 6 June. It was impossible to turn back now. Thus the only thing to do was to liquidate Heindrich before he got into the train. Although no one in the Prime Minister's entourage saw how this could be done now, Buck admitted that he still had a joker to play.

Suzy and Jeanne

Shortly before three p.m., Melchior arrived at the apartment in the rue Élisée-Reclus. Louise had given him Eddy's address, and after the failure of the operation in the metro, he thought the members of the commando would be there, since they had no other secure hideout.

No one answered when he knocked on the door. Fearing for a moment that he'd come too late, Melchior forced the lock and entered the apartment. 'Jeanne? Suzy? Are you there?' he asked in a loud voice.

He had no sooner shut the door than he found himself face-to-face with a pistol barrel. Jeanne, her eyes bulging, was pointing it at him and trembling. Not far from her, Suzy and Eddy, also armed, had just opened the service door.

'Who are you? How did you know our names?' Jeanne asked, cocking her pistol. Melchior identified himself. He explained that he had got Louise's rifle for her, and was working for Buck. He knew that Suzy had a meeting with Heindrich at six p.m. While he was talking, Eddy quickly frisked him and took his pistol.

'How do you know all that? How do I know you're not a Boche sent by Heindrich?' Jeanne said, taking a step towards him.

'The concierge at the Regina is one of ours. Heindrich informed him that he was expecting a young woman, and asked him to have her come up to room 813.'

Eddy looked at Jeanne, shaking his head. Suzy remembered hearing Louise talk to Maria about a certain Melchior. But Jeanne was still not convinced.

'Heindrich must not come out of that room alive. I've come to help you,' Melchior concluded, still holding his hands up.

'What do you propose?'

'First of all, to take you somewhere else. You mustn't stay here. My car is parked down below. Hurry, we don't have much time.'

Melchior took them to the museum, where he explained his plan in great detail. Thanks to contacts inside the hotel, Jeanne, disguised as a chambermaid, would hide a pistol underneath the pillow, so that Suzy could get her hands on it quickly when Heindrich had joined her. Suzy was to shoot her former lover twice in the head, and then jump out the window, where a large hamper full of laundry would cushion her fall. Jeanne would then take her to a car driven by Eddy.

'Do you have questions?' Melchior asked when he had finished.

Suzy, who had not yet opened her mouth, decided to speak. 'I could never do that.'

In consternation, they all turned to look at her. 'But you said you'd kill him!' Jeanne cried.

'I will. But I can't jump out the window,' Suzy admitted.

Jeanne was speechless. Melchior took off his spectacles; he seemed suddenly to have aged ten years. 'It's the only way to evacuate you, Suzy,' he said. 'You'll have only a few seconds.'

'I'll find a way.'

Jeanne took her hand and pressed it very hard. Suzy lowered her eyes. She said nothing more, but everyone understood the choice she'd just made.

At 5.55 that afternoon, Suzy entered the revolving door at the Regina. Dressed in a white dress and wearing a navy blue hat with a veil, she tried to follow the orders Melchior had given her:

concentrate on a single detail from the moment she entered the hotel until she had arrived at room 813. But images from the past rose up in her despite herself. She saw herself making the same trip two years earlier, on Karl's arm. She'd had a great deal of champagne and stumbled several times, clinging to him. Each time he had vigorously held her up. His somewhat feminine laugh had surprised her in a man with such authority.

In the lobby, the decoration had been changed; the furniture was more rococo. Suzy liked the new wing chairs. She tried to concentrate on the shape of their arms. When she got to the reception desk, she leaned against the counter and collected her wits. She did not immediately notice the concierge bending towards her.

'Mademoiselle Liliane?'

Suzy looked up. The man was looking at her with a smile.

'You're expected in room 813. Follow the attendant, he'll escort you.'

'I know my way, thank you ...'

'Colonel Heindrich asked that you be taken there.'

A few metres to her right, the attendant was waiting near the lift. Suzy was starting towards him when a soldier stepped in front of her and searched her. Her heartbeat accelerated. She remembered that Karl had done the same thing on their first night, at exactly the same spot, but in a joking way. Careless and happy, she had laughed uproariously, never imagining that two years later she would find herself at the same place, about to commit her first and last murder.

Entering the lift, she thought again about the question Gaëlle had asked her in the van just after they'd evacuated the British geologist. What were they going to do if they got back to London alive? She had replied that she wanted to dance in a great hall with

164

her name written in large letters on the billboard. Now that idea seemed very infantile. What would she do if she survived Karl's murder? The obvious response came to her as the attendant was pushing the button for the second floor: she would go to Liverpool to see her son. Not to introduce herself to him, or even to talk to him, but just to watch him from a distance, without his adoptive parents being aware of her presence. She concentrated on this idea until the attendant opened the door to room 813.

Nothing in the room had changed since the last time. It was redolent of the same perfume, and the flowers in the vases seemed identical. The morbid atmosphere of the room made her shiver. She stood by the window and lit a cigarette. In the courtyard, she could see the laundry hamper. She closed her eyes and exhaled the smoke through her nostrils. Someone knocked at the door. Suzy started, and extinguished her cigarette. For a brief moment, she didn't know how to act. But it was not Karl at the door. Jeanne came into the room to bring her clean sheets. And the pistol, which she placed under the pillow.

The two women exchanged a long look, and then Jeanne turned on her heel without a word. Suzy went up to the bed and put her hand under the pillow. She took out the revolver, which looked enormous to her. Her arm trembled slightly; the weapon felt heavy. How would she be able to fire? Footsteps approached in the corridor. She put the pistol in her handbag and went back to the window. A few seconds later, the door to the room opened and a man came in whom Suzy could identify by his walk and his breathing: Karl. He was as wrought up as she was, perhaps even more. He came closer to her and stood just behind her. Suzy tensed all her muscles, because she sensed that he was looking at the nape of her neck. She'd put her hair in a chignon – on purpose, because that was how she'd usually worn it when they went out together. Heindrich first put his hand on her neck, then moved up to her skull, where he stopped. Only then did she hear him speak.

'I never believed you were dead, you know.'

She turned round to face him, her features still hidden behind her veil. He was looking into her eyes now. He had aged; wrinkles had appeared round his eyes, and his complexion was muddier. Suzy thought about Liverpool, and she clung to that image, which at that moment seemed to her the only promise of a future she could make her own. She slipped her hand into her bag and gripped the handle of the revolver, which already seemed less large to her.

'Why did you leave, Liliane?'

'It … would never have worked.'

Karl stared at her as if he were trying to read between the lines. She was holding the pistol in her hand, all she had to do was take it out of the bag and point it at him. 'Shoot twice,' Melchior had said. But she thought her former lover was too close to her.

'Give us a second chance. Come with me to Germany, I'm leaving this evening.'

Suzy shook her head, and Karl, surprised, drew away from her. Suzy took out the pistol and aimed it at him. He didn't seem taken aback, which made her uneasy.

'Is it Buckmaster who sent you? Are you part of the commando?' he asked. 'What did they promise you in exchange?'

Suzy cocked the pistol, but her hand began to tremble. She couldn't pull the trigger.

'What we had was beautiful, Liliane. Don't let them spoil it.'

Unable to control her feelings any longer, Suzy lowered her pistol and turned her face away. Karl took her in his arms and was already trying to kiss her, his hand on the pistol that she was still holding. Suzy gave herself up to him, pressing her lips to Karl's. He picked her up and carried her to the bed, where he covered her body with his. Her head buried in the pillows, Suzy let go of the pistol and put her legs around Karl. But at the moment he entered her, she had a moment of lucidity. The look he gave her suddenly seemed unbearable. Karl, overcome by his passion, didn't see her seize the pistol.

Jeanne was still on the third-floor landing when she heard the shots. Two very brief cracks, just as Melchior had asked, and then nothing. Down below, two men were already climbing the stairs, shouting. Jeanne ran to the room; the door was still closed. Before the soldiers arrived on the floor, Jeanne had disappeared. The chaos ignited by the gunfire allowed her to return to the courtyard without hindrance. Seeing the laundry hamper, she realized that Suzy had not jumped. Still dressed in her chambermaid's clothes, she hurried to leave the hotel by the service entrance, and then got into the car, where Eddy and Melchior were waiting.

'Let's clear out, quick!' she cried, taking off her apron.

Melchior looked at her, his pistol in his hand. Sitting behind the wheel, Eddy hesitated. 'What about Suzy?'

Jeanne was about to answer when there was shouting at the door of the hotel. Two nurses appeared with a stretcher on which a body was lying. A white sheet covered the corpse, making it impossible to see who it was.

In the car, the three members of the commando held their breath. The nurses loaded the stretcher into the back of a van before climbing in after it. Behind them, another group came out of the hotel. A man walked in front, his face pale but his step firm. Heindrich. He kept walking, but his eyes followed the van, which was pulling away. He put on his cap and got into his car. Jeanne plunged her face into her hands.

'Damn, we failed, he's all right. Drive!' she commanded.

Eddy pushed gently on the accelerator, and the car entered the rue de Rivoli. Jeanne was weeping silently; Melchior offered her his shoulder.

'There's only one way now,' he murmured, staring into space.

Louise

Chained up in the Gestapo's offices, Pierre and Louise remained silent. The presence of their torturers left them no privacy, but they wouldn't have talked in any case. What they felt for each other at that moment went far beyond words.

In trading his sister's life for the secret of 'Phoenix', Pierre had realized how unbearable her death would have been for him, even more so than defeat in the war and the sacrifice of thousands. His betrayal, which proceeded from his senseless love, revealed the unconscious domination she'd exercised over him for years. What his confession said to her was, 'I'm talking because I can't imagine a world in which you don't exist.' Louise was angry with herself for not having loved this brother. Her excessive strength of character had led him to the most terrible of weaknesses. She'd never given him a chance to make a place for himself.

Suddenly Heindrich appeared, ashen in the wan light. His eyes were red, he seemed dazed, and in general he looked like a prisoner on his way to the scaffold. Only one person could have thrown him into such distress, Louise thought. Suzy.

His eyes full of hatred, the colonel put his face very close to Louise's, and she smelled the alcohol on his breath. The man seemed devastated. He spat in her face.

'You shouldn't have used Liliane. You're responsible for her death.' The torturers were struck dumb. Heindrich kept his bulging eyes fixed on Louise. Volker had now come in.

'You're going to be transferred to La Roquette prison,' Heindrich continued. 'I'm taking your brother with me to Germany. This is the last time you'll see each other.'

Louise turned to Pierre. She was having a hard time holding back her tears. He was smiling at her, his face strangely serene.

Heindrich ordered his men to unbind the prisoners. On a low table, Pierre had noticed a scalpel. When his wrists had finally been freed, he lunged for the scalpel and cut his own throat in a rapid movement. The wall was sprayed with blood. Louise lurched towards him but was held back by the guards. Totally dazed, Heindrich watched as Volker tried in vain to stop the haemorrhaging, but the artery was deeply cut and it was clear that nothing could be done. Pierre died with a smile on his lips before the eyes of his sister, who was shaking with sobs. It was going to be much harder to convince Rommel without Pierre present.

'Kill me too,' Louise begged. 'I'm asking you that as a favour.'

Trembling slightly, Heindrich came up to her for the last time. 'I've only one favour to offer you. You can choose between deportation to Germany and execution.'

'I choose execution.'

'I'll see to it.'

A few hours later, Louise was taken to the Fresnes prison. A firing squad was supposed to execute her as soon as she arrived. Sitting in the semi-darkness of the lorry, watched by a guard, she suddenly felt an acute pain shoot through her abdomen. The blows she'd received during the interrogation must have hurt the foetus. Louise thought that her baby might also be expressing his anger at being sacrificed by a mother who had put other interests before his. Her thoughts then turned to Claude, Gaëlle, Suzy, Maria and Pierre, whom she was going to join without feeling the slightest fear. For the first time, death seemed to her a deliverance. She had more friends among the dead than among the living. She regretted nothing, except having not killed Heindrich in the metro. Louise recalled her doubts on the way to the Institute for the Blind. Should she have run away rather than continuing with the mission? She thought about that question for a long time without finding an answer.

Crossing the Bois de Boulogne, the lorry suddenly slowed and stopped for no apparent reason. Louise heard several gunshots in front of the vehicle, while another burst broke the lock on its rear door. Before he could even resist, the guard was cut down by a new volley. Melchior appeared, submachine-gun in hand, and despite the smoke Louise saw him signal her to hurry. She jumped up and managed to get out, despite the shackles on her ankles. Then she saw Jeanne, wearing a German uniform and cap and holding a pistol. They fell into each other's arms. Melchior reminded them that they didn't have much time. Eddy backed the car up to meet them. Melchior opened the boot and took out a grey uniform, which he handed to Louise. This disguise would help her cross the barrier at the Gare de l'Est.

'We have to stop Heindrich. A plane is waiting in Orléans to take you to London. It will be there until midnight. Eddy knows exactly where it is.'

By means of a couple of precisely aimed shots, Jeanne freed Louise from her shackles, and they were all getting ready to get in the car when they suddenly heard a shot behind them. Melchior stiffened, a thin thread of blood dripping from the corner of his lip. He fell to his knees, revealing the guard from the lorry, who was staggering towards them, his pistol in his hand. Jeanne riddled him with bullets. Louise prevented her from emptying her magazine into a man who was already dead. 'Come on, let's go,' she breathed. Her eyes shining with an unusual light, Jeanne looked at Melchior's body for the last time. Then the car drove off at high speed.

On the platform from which the train to Berlin was to leave, a large military deployment was in place. Standing on the steps of the first-class carriage, Heindrich was finishing a cigarette. He looked at his watch. More than six minutes until departure. He inhaled a last puff for the pleasure of feeling the smoke enter his lungs. On the opposite platform, a train had just stopped, and he could clearly see a whole series of numbers painted on the first carriage. The cigarette still in his mouth, Karl couldn't resist the temptation to add up all these figures and try to reduce them to his lucky number. But the result was the number five, which displeased him. However, he didn't doubt that he would be able to convince Rommel despite Pierre's absence. He was now sure of succeeding. He understood that he would have to stop believing in signs. Omens reflected nothing but his own insecurity. And now he felt sure of himself as never before.

Wearing her uniform, Louise appeared at the head of the platform. Jeanne, dressed in civilian clothes, followed her, accompanied by Eddy, who was obviously terrified. When Louise handed her pass to the ticket-puncher, she was denied access to the train.

'But I have papers that Colonel Heindrich must sign before he leaves. It's very important,' she protested, showing the man some documents. The guard refused even to look at them. Heindrich had given very strict orders, and the only people who were to be allowed to cross the barrier were travellers with tickets.

For a moment, Louise and Jeanne didn't know what to do, and exchanged a worried look. On their right a drunken German soldier on leave was hugging a girl and talking loudly. Jeanne stared at him, and her eyes suddenly took on the fire they'd had in the Bois de Boulogne when Melchior collapsed. Her face very pale, she put her hand in the pocket of her raincoat and whispered to Louise, 'Go ahead, run, and don't worry about me.'

Jeanne turned and aimed her pistol at the tipsy soldier and put two bullets in his head. Everyone around them panicked at the sound of the shots. The guards supervising access to the platform rushed towards her to disarm her, and Jeanne didn't resist them. A smile on her lips, she met her friend's eyes for the last time just as Louise was pushing through the barrier. Handcuffed and flanked by two sturdy soldiers, Jeanne noticed Eddy in the crowd, his face full of surprise and admiration.

Heindrich had also heard the shots, but being too far from the barrier he couldn't see anything. Over the loudspeakers, a voice announced the departure of the train for Berlin. Heindrich threw away his cigarette end and was getting ready to board the train when he noticed a silhouette in uniform coming towards him on his right.

'Colonel, wait a moment, please.'

Before his brain realized that he knew that voice, the barrel of the silencer coughed twice and Karl staggered, a terrible burning in his back. On his knees, clutching the step, he saw the holes in his uniform, the bullets having pierced his chest. Suffocating, he looked

173

at the silhouette facing him. When Louise was sure that she had correctly identified him, she put two more bullets in his head. Thrown violently backwards, Heindrich rolled under the carriage and landed near his still smoking cigarette end. Louise disappeared as the wheels of the carriage began to roll over the German's body.

Leaving the station, Louise was afraid she wouldn't be able to find Eddy. The soldiers might have identified him and taken him away along with Jeanne. Going back to his car was risky, but she hardly had a choice. Without showing how feverish she was, Louise walked around the area in front of the station until she found Eddy's car, which was parked down below. She saw him sitting at the wheel, weeping. Around him everything was calm. Jeanne must still have been occupying most of the soldiers inside the station. After checking that no one was watching her, Louise went down the steps and got into the car beside Eddy.

'There's nothing more we can do for her. Let's go, the plane won't wait any longer.'

Dazed, Eddy stared at her for a few seconds. When Louise asked him what he was waiting for, he pointed to the rear-view mirror. Louise saw her reflection; Heindrich's blood had spurted onto her uniform and her chin without her even having noticed it.

They started out slowly, and then took the road towards Orléans, where they arrived only a few minutes before the plane's departure. Louise urged Eddy to get on the plane with her, but he surprised her by choosing to remain. Because of his past behaviour, he was afraid of being put in prison by the British and not being able to defend himself because he didn't know their language.

'But you helped me, nothing will happen to you. I'll talk for you,' Louise protested.

Eddy stuck to his decision, but he argued that he deserved a share of the money for his contribution to Heindrich's execution. In a burst of generosity, Louise gave him all the money and then wished him good luck. As the plane took off, she looked out the window and saw Eddy running back to his car with the valise. What sort of life would he have in France now? She was never to find out.

During the flight, Louise once again felt shooting pains in her abdomen. Taking off her raincoat, she saw blood running down her legs. She was forced to lie down on the floor. The pilot, who didn't know what was going on, gave her worried looks from time to time. The sudden reduction in tension resulting from the end of the mission must have triggered a miscarriage. Desperate, Louise broke down in tears, while the bleeding between her thighs increased. Since she had escaped from the lorry, she had been under no illusions about the baby's fate, but the sudden confrontation with reality caused a surge of emotion that almost killed her. The plane finally landed at the Aldershot military airfield. Louise, inert, was rushed to the military hospital, where she received emergency care. In a semi-coma, she heard someone asking if she wanted to talk to a clergyman. She declined and slipped into a dreamless sleep.

When she awoke in the early dawn, Louise was surprised to find Buckmaster at her bedside. He'd been sitting there silently for several hours. Seeing her eyes open, he took her hand. 'I'm sorry about Pierre. And I learned about your baby.'

She looked at him without saying anything. What could she say, anyway?

'The landing will take place as planned,' Buck went on. 'I talked with the Prime Minister on the telephone a little while ago. He wants to congratulate you personally, you and Jeanne.'

This time Louise could not keep silent. 'Tell him that if that's what he wants, he'll have to bring Jeanne back to England. I'm counting on him to do that. Personally.'

Buck didn't move for a few seconds. Louise's grim face had cut short any expression of enthusiasm. The colonel just nodded and left the room.

Afterwards

Louise went to live at Pierre's house in London. Buck found her work as a nurse in a hospital for soldiers seriously wounded during the invasion of Normandy. For about a year, she took care of men who were half dead. The least badly injured of them told her about the horror of the fighting. Modestly, she listened to them in silence, without ever mentioning the pain that she had borne within her every day for months. Churchill had called her personally to express his admiration for her and to thank her for having contributed to the Allied landing. Without seeming moved, Louise had replied that the success would be complete only when Jeanne Faussier returned. After a pause, he'd promised that every effort would be made to find her.

In early May 1945, while attending a showing of *Gone with the Wind*, Louise saw a newsreel about the American army's liberation of the Buchenwald concentration camp. The soldiers had filmed the mass graves they'd found when they arrived there. The surrealistic images of bodies piled on top of one another passed in front of the shocked audience. One shot gave Louise a jolt when she saw a scaffold from which GIs were removing a woman who had recently been hanged. The woman's naked, lacerated body was frighteningly emaciated, but Louise immediately recognized Jeanne. In the middle of the crowded cinema, she broke down in tears. A woman sitting next to her took her in her arms to comfort her, but Louise abruptly got up and went home. She remained prostrate there for a full day.

A week later, Buck confirmed Jeanne's death. She had been deported shortly after her arrest at the Gare de l'Est, and executed only a few hours before the Allies arrived. Louise recalled their first meeting, at Luton prison, where Jeanne was already about to mount the scaffold. By proposing that she join their mission, Louise had simply delayed an execution that the prisoner could not escape. Louise was well aware that Jeanne had saved her life. Now she knew what she had to do to honour Jeanne's memory, and that of all those she had left behind. But she waited for the right moment, out of respect for a promise she'd made in a van on a remote road in Normandy, so long ago.

On the night of 8 May 1945, Louise was on duty at the hospital when the surrender was signed. The whole staff listened to the Prime Minister's speech on the radio. A few patients were awakened for the occasion. To everyone's astonishment, the news was met with a respectful silence. They all looked at each other, torn between laughter and tears. Louise did not weep, but neither did she feel inclined to rejoice. She had dreamed about this moment for years, and now that it had finally arrived, she was almost indifferent. Sitting on a chair off to the side, she placed her nurse's cap on her knees and closed her eyes. She was surprised to find herself wondering if it had been worth all that she'd lost. She no longer had anyone with whom she could celebrate this victory she'd been waiting for so long, no child to whom she could give it as a promise. Heindrich's face at the railway station passed before her eyes for the first time in months. It was less his dazed countenance than his cigarette end burning on the ground that she saw. She remembered it with such precision that she could have counted the grey stripes on its white paper.

She had won the war and now was thinking about a cigarette. She had to get out; suddenly it was too hot.

'Louise, where are you off to? You can't leave now, we're going to celebrate,' one of her co-workers said.

'I'm going to bed. I'm tired,' she replied to the stupefaction of everyone.

She slept deeply for six hours, despite the din in the streets. When she woke up, she took a bath, then got dressed without eating anything at all; her mind was completely occupied by the task that remained for her to do. As she buttoned her trenchcoat to go out, she noticed that her hand was trembling slightly.

Outside, there were still crowds milling about. From their windows, people were throwing showers of confetti that fell on her indifferent shoulders. No one had slept, and yet Louise seemed the most exhausted. Making her way through the crowd, she received a dozen embraces, to which she did not respond.

Not sharing in the happiness that surrounded her, Louise walked to the closest Anglican church. Its open doors were a kind of invitation. However, once she had crossed the threshold Louise hesitated. She hadn't been in a church for more than five years, and the dozen metres separating her from the altar suddenly seemed impossible to traverse. Louise nonetheless surprised herself by walking up the central aisle without faltering even once. After crossing herself before the altar, she lit five candles without shedding a single tear.

She took a few steps back to look at the flickering flames. Then she knelt down and, in the silence, began to pray for Pierre Desfontaines and for Maria, Gaëlle, Suzy and Jeanne, her sister agents.